W9-AWC-571

Dear Reader,

We're constantly striving to bring you the best
romance fiction by the most exciting authors...
and in Harlequin Romance® we're especially keen
to feature fresh, sparkling, warmly emotional novels.
Modern love stories to suit your every mood: poignant,
deeply moving stories; lively, upbeat romances with
sparks flying; or sophisticated, edgy novels with an
international flavor.

All our authors are special, and we hope you
continue to enjoy each month's new selection of
Harlequin Romance books. This month we're delighted
to feature a novel with extra fizz! New Australian
author Ally Blake sparkles with a fresh, vivid and lively
writing style, and *The Wedding Wish* simply effervesces
with vibrant, witty, lovable characters such as Holly
and Jake—but also their friends Beth, Ben and Lydia.
It's fresh, flirty and feel-good!

We hope you enjoy this book by Ally Blake—and look
out for future sparkling stories in Harlequin Romance.
If you'd like to share your thoughts and comments
with us, do please write to:

The Harlequin Romance® Editors
Harlequin Mills & Boon Ltd.
Eton House
18-24 Paradise Road
Richmond
Surrey TW9 1SR, U.K.
or e-mail: www.Tango@hmb.co.uk

Happy reading!

The Editors

NO RETURN

Ally Blake worked in retail, danced on television and acted in friends' short films until the writing bug could no longer be ignored. And as her mother had read romance novels ever since Ally was a baby, the aspiration to write Harlequin novels had been almost bred into her. Ally married her gorgeous husband, Mark, in Las Vegas (no Elvis in sight, thank you very much) and they live in beautiful Melbourne, Australia. Her husband cooks, he cleans and he's the love of her life. How's that for a hero?

This is Ally Blake's first book!

THE WEDDING WISH

Ally Blake

TANGO
IT TAKES TWO...

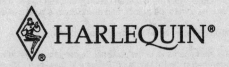

HARLEQUIN®

TORONTO • NEW YORK • LONDON
AMSTERDAM • PARIS • SYDNEY • HAMBURG
STOCKHOLM • ATHENS • TOKYO • MILAN • MADRID
PRAGUE • WARSAW • BUDAPEST • AUCKLAND

This book is dedicated to my angel, Mark,
who looked after me, brought me M&M's
and made me feel as if I had it in me all the time.

ISBN 0-373-03782-1

THE WEDDING WISH

First North American Publication 2004.

CHAPTER ONE

'I'M GETTING married,' Holly announced as she slammed her briefcase on the desk in her office at Cloud Nine Event Management, fifteen minutes later than her usual start time.

'You're doing what?' Beth's voice rang metallic and loud from Holly's speakerphone.

Holly sat down, crossed her legs, noticed a run in her stockings, and her mood went from bad to worse. She grabbed a new pair of stockings from the neat pile stocked in her bottom desk drawer, before moving into her private bathroom to change from frayed to fresh. She had to raise her voice for it to reach the speakerphone, but in her current temper that was not a problem.

'I said I'm getting married.'

'But I can't remember you dating any man more than once in the last six months, much less becoming familiar enough to want to *marry* one of them.'

Holly's assistant Lydia chose that moment to enter the office. She stopped in her tracks, the coffee she carried all but sloshing over the sides, and stared at the speakerphone as though it had produced an offensive noise. Holly came back into the room, new stockings in place, and waved a 'hurry up' hand at Lydia who placed the cup down without spilling a drop.

With no apology, Lydia joined the private conversation. 'Did I hear you guys right? In the time it took for me to make Holly a cuppa, she's hooked herself a fiancé? That's saying something for instant coffee.'

'Is that you, Lydia?' Beth asked.

Lydia leaned towards the speakerphone, articulating her words as though speaking to someone hard of hearing. 'How are you, Beth? When is the baby due?'

'I'm fantastic. Baby Jeffries should be here in a month or so—'

'Ah, guys,' Holly interrupted, 'major life decision being made here.'

Lydia mimed buttoning her lips shut tight.

'Sorry, sweetie,' Beth said. 'Blame Lydia. You know if anyone asks about the bubby, I gush. Do go on.'

'Thank you.' Holly took a deep breath and launched into her story. 'This morning, as I walked the last block along Lonsdale Street, this...*man* all but barrelled me over. Everything I was carrying went flying. My briefcase ended up in the gutter, pens rolled down the road and all my precious papers scattered across the footpath. And as I was on my hands and knees crawling around collecting my materials *he* had the nerve to tell *me* to watch where *I* was going.'

'Was he cute?' was Lydia's instant response.

Not cute, Holly remembered. She pictured early morning sunlight glinting off light flecks in hazel eyes. Tired dark smudges underneath those eyes. Sympathy she had felt at his exhausted expression. His scowl as he had realised she had dropped everything she was carrying. The same scowl that had extinguished her sympathy. The rich, deep voice with a hint of a foreign accent as he had said his piece. No, cute was not the word.

'Tall,' Holly eventually established, 'dark mussed hair. Matching dimples. Smelled nice. But that's irrelevant.'

'Irrelevant?' Beth said. 'He sounds perfect.'

'I reckon,' Lydia agreed.

'Just when you stop looking where you are going, he finds you. It's kismet.'

Holly rolled her eyes, picturing Beth reaching for one of her New Age books to justify the incident.

'He did not find me, Beth, he berated and bruised me. See.' Holly pointed out a light scrape on her knee to Lydia, who pouted in appreciation.

'And this is the guy you're going to marry?' Lydia asked.

'No! You've both missed the point.'

'Which is?'

'The point is, the whole horrible episode brought about an epiphany. My social life consists exclusively of attending parties we coordinate. But instead of meeting men, I meet male party personalities. They mislead me with an attractive, charming, confident disguise but there is never anything *more* going on behind the eye-catching masks they wear. The *gentleman* this morning was very attractive, uncompromising, and uncaring and was therefore the embodiment of all that is wrong with the men I meet. It's a foolproof theory.'

'I'm confused,' Lydia said. 'If not this guy, who on earth are you marrying?'

'That's the thing—I've decided Ben is going to find him for me.'

'My Ben?' Beth asked after a couple of seconds of bewildered silence.

'Of course. Can't you see it's the only way? Ben works in a big company, he's got plenty of staff under him, mostly young men he has hand-picked, and he knows me better than anyone apart from you guys. He's the perfect objective observer and if he can find me someone he likes then we can all be friends for ever. You know, live next door to one another, have neighbourhood BBQs, go on camping trips…'

'You hate camping—'

'I'm not joking, Beth. Come on, you have to see how flawless a plan it is.'

'And all of this came from banging into some very attractive, dimpled, nice smelling guy on the street?' Beth asked.

'It was like when we collided he smacked some sense into me.'

'Gave you concussion, more like it,' Lydia muttered.

Holly shot Lydia an unimpressed look.

'This guy must have been something to get you of all people talking marriage,' Beth said.

'Why me of all people?'

'Come on, Holly. You are the most controlled, independent woman I know. You keep a colour range of spare pairs of stockings in your office drawer, for goodness' sake.'

Catching sight of those very packets, Holly casually closed the drawer shut with her foot.

'And here you are,' Beth continued, 'wanting to put your future happiness in someone else's hands.'

'Ben is not just someone else and you know that. I trust him to make a good choice.'

'I can't believe you are making some sort of sense,' Beth admitted. 'All right, come over for dinner tonight so that we can ambush my poor, unknowing husband.'

'Thanks, Beth. You are the best friend in the whole wide world.'

'And don't you forget it.'

After Beth rang off Lydia peeled her lanky form from the chair and loped to Holly's office door where she turned back to ask, 'Did he help pick the stuff up?'

Holly dragged her attention away from the beckoning projects on her desk. 'Mmm, he dropped his bags and bent down to help almost instantly. But he was telling me off at the time so that's irrelevant too.'

'And you were walking with your head down, immersed in thoughts of what you had to do today, not looking where you were going, weren't you?'

'Sure…'

'But that's irrelevant, right?'

Holly narrowed her eyes, willing Lydia not to continue, but her mocking look was to no avail.

'A tall, dark, handsome stranger bowls you over and then gets down on his hands and knees to help. And you have decided this is a bad thing. I, on the other hand, would spend the rest of the day looking dreamily out the window if that happened to me. But no such luck. My morning consisted of being rubbed up against by a school-boy on the train.'

Lydia sighed spectacularly and Holly could not help but grin at her amateur dramatics. 'You do realise that since I am your boss your job is to ooh and aah and say, ''poor Holly'', don't you?'

'I thought my job was to get you coffee and stand on chairs so that you can drape fabrics over me and hold all incoming calls from any men you may have had uninspir-ing dates with the night before.'

'Sure,' Holly agreed after a moment's thought, 'that too.'

Lydia left the room and headed back to her desk to prepare herself for a day of imagining walking up Lonsdale Street and banging into tall, dark, handsome strangers.

Jacob helped the driver haul the last of his luggage into the waiting taxi. As the car pulled away he ran a hand through his mussed hair, leant back onto the headrest, and was surprised to catch such a world-weary reflection peering back at him from the window.

Jacob's focus shifted and he watched the familiar hometown buildings flick past. He was not yet sure how he felt about being home. So far, so good. And a hot shower and a sleep in his own bed would only make it better. But how long would it be this time before he yearned to move on?

Either way Jacob knew Melbourne was a magnificent city. Take that enchanting woman he had just had an exchange with on the street. Now there was a real Melbourne woman. Pale smooth skin suited to the temperate clime, stylish to a fault, a compelling face, and subtle, easy confidence. You didn't find women quite like that anywhere else in the world. In any case he hadn't yet. During the drive home, his thoughts kept coming back to the brunette with the fiery blue eyes who had somehow roused his ordinarily controlled temper.

Jet lag. It had to have been jet lag.

'Babe?' Ben's voice called out from the front hallway.

Holly's hand leapt to her throat. She had not even heard the front door.

'In here, darling,' Beth called, sitting on an armchair they'd dragged into the kitchen to ease her aching back.

Holly understood Beth's raised eyebrows and tight mouth. *This is your last chance to change your mind,* her expression said. But Holly was not to be deterred. 'Just follow the delicious aroma of grilled chicken à la Holly wafting from the kitchen.'

Ben popped his head around the door. He leaned down and kissed his wife, not even asking why their lounge chair was in the kitchen. Holly offered her cheek for a kiss, which she duly received.

'To what do we owe the pleasure of your company,

gorgeous?' Ben leant over Holly to have a good look at dinner. She slapped his hand as he tried to grab a piece of potato.

Holly glanced once more at Beth, who gave her a discreet thumbs up. 'I want you to set me up with someone from your work.'

Holly clenched her face waiting for the inevitable 'no'.

'Sure,' Ben answered.

Holly was too stunned to stop him spooning a baby potato into his mouth. 'Really?'

'Of course. It's Derek from Payroll, isn't it? He's always had a thing for you, you know.'

'For starters it's not Derek. I mean, yuck.'

'Come on, Ben,' Beth said in support, 'you know she likes tall, dark and handsome. Derek's a weed.'

'Then who?'

Holly proceeded to explain her inspired theory and the mechanics of her plan with endlessly increasing enthusiasm until Ben could have no doubt of her sincerity.

'You two are serious, aren't you?'

'Deadly serious,' Beth agreed. 'I have mapped out her stars, and Holly is primed.'

Ben did a Groucho Marx with his eyebrows. Beth slapped his thigh playfully. 'Primed for a big change, you idiot. This is serious, Ben. She is getting on in years.'

'She's twenty-seven.'

'And I want to be her matron of honour while I'm still young enough and pretty enough to at least have a shot at outshining the bride.'

'You're nuts, the both of you. I shouldn't let the two of you alone in a room together. It bodes badly for the future of mankind.'

'But you will do it, won't you, darling?'

Faced with their excited united front, there was nothing Ben could do but agree.

CHAPTER TWO

SO, THE next night Holly meandered through the outer bar of the Fun and Games sports nightclub on the arm of her best friend's husband. She was dressed to kill in a black silk dress: fitted, strapless and split to the thigh.

'Do you have anyone in particular lined up for me tonight?' Holly shouted in Ben's ear to be heard over the loud, pumping music.

'Actually, I stuck your photo on the wall in the men's washroom at work along with a note saying you would be here tonight. That way they can just come to you.'

'Not funny.' Holly punched Ben inelegantly in the arm. 'Why is the function here?'

'It's one of ours. It's Link's idea. We hold all of our functions in various clubs we own so we are constantly reinvesting in ourselves.'

Holly nodded, impressed. 'Ingenious. Pity all Lincoln Holdings events are managed internally. I could have a lot of fun with the budget you guys must have.' She huddled closer. 'Will the boss be here tonight?'

'Link? Sorry, Holly, you can cross him off your list. He's been running the international operations from New Orleans for the last few years.'

'I bet he's tall, dark, and handsome to boot.' Holly pouted, bringing a smile to Ben's face. The smile probably meant his boss was a married workaholic with three whining kids, a pot-belly and high blood pressure.

He took her hand and led her single file through the swelling crowd, into the private function room hidden at the rear of the club. The room had been converted into a sort of theatre in the round. The high ceiling housed an elaborate lighting rig so bright it was almost blinding.

A cheerful murmur of voices and clinking drinking glasses echoing in the lofty space had replaced the raucous club music, soundproof walls thankfully shutting out the thumping beat from the previous room.

Holly excused herself several times as they edged past people sitting in their row. The numerous men in dinner suits sent a thrill of excitement running up and down her spine. She sat and turned to Ben, ready to ask what was behind the velvet floor-to-ceiling drapes in the centre of the room but her query froze on her lips. The curtains slowly rose into the rafters to reveal— A boxing ring!

Ben chatted to a couple of male colleagues in the row in front. Their eyes all gleamed like little boys in a pet store as they launched into a detailed discussion of the two men who were about to belt it out before them.

Holly tugged on Ben's sleeve. 'There's a boxing ring.'

He smiled. 'That's so that the boxers keep to themselves and don't spill out into the crowd.'

'But, I thought…I thought this was a business function. I thought we'd be sitting down, having dinner, and there would be refined and elegant men for you to introduce to me.'

'We're sitting. We're eating,' Ben said with a mouthful of mixed nuts he had picked up from a nattily dressed wandering waiter. 'And this is Mark and Jeremy.'

The mundane middle-aged guys from the row in front smiled politely.

Ben's twinkling eyes fast lost their twinkle when Holly grabbed him gracelessly by the lapels of his tuxedo jacket and through clenched teeth said, 'But this was not what I had in mind.'

'Just relax. You'll enjoy it.'

Holly raised her eyebrows, pursed her lips and crossed her arms, demonstrating exactly how much she was enjoying the night so far. 'I am surprised that Lincoln Holdings would associate itself with such a primitive and politically incorrect enterprise.'

'All of Lincoln Holdings' staff from the managing directors to the custodial staff come together for these nights. It makes inter-office difficulties seem so small and petty when compared with what these guys go through to earn a living. You should know more than anyone that if a gimmick works, stick with it.'

'It's not just a gimmick, Ben, it's encouraging people to use their fists to sort out their differences. Whose idea was this in the first place?'

'Link's, of course,' Ben said, grinning. 'Forever inspirational.'

'Sounds like a thug to me,' Holly muttered.

'You thought he was ingenious ten minutes ago.'

'Ten minutes ago I was mistaken.'

Holly was suddenly glad that Ben's boss would not be at the function. If he were, she would have no problems letting him know what she thought of his little soirée, high blood pressure or no high blood pressure.

And she just knew that sitting quietly at home in her 'magic' briefcase—as Lydia called it—she would have a dozen more appropriate and inspirational function ideas and it frustrated her to distraction.

The white noise of the murmuring crowd rose to a crescendo when an announcer in black tie bounded into the ring and a microphone descended from the rafters. The crowd rose to its collective feet and Holly rose with it, shuffling her way back out of their row in search of a refuge.

Once inside the ladies' room, she slumped down on a very large round pink velvet ottoman, which sat alone in the middle of the vast space.

Her eyes were closed and she was plotting ways she could take revenge on Ben when the doors swung open. She opened her eyes, hoping to find solace with another woman in the same predicament as herself, but instead locked eyes with the least feminine person she had ever seen.

In walked a man well over six feet tall, his tuxedo precisely tailored to fit his athletic frame. He was so stunning it took her breath away. Maybe this night would not be a complete waste after all.

And then something about the furrowed brow and deep hazel eyes clicked in her memory. His neat, freshly cut hair framing his handsome, relaxed face had momentarily blinded her to the fact that she knew him.

He was the same brute who had knocked her down in the street the day before!

Her senses surged to full alert. He radiated charisma, confidence and composure. Any other girl would find it near impossible to stand firm against that killer combination of attributes.

But Holly was not just any other girl. Holly had protection. Holly had a foolproof theory and Holly had Ben to keep just this sort of guy beneath her radar.

So where was Ben now she really needed him? Hmm. No Ben. She and her theory would have to fend for themselves. And her foremost plan was to make the brute leave the room before he recognised her.

She shot to her feet, holding her clutch purse in front of her chest as a shield and said, 'Excuse me, this is the ladies' room.'

The man stopped short at her words.

'Actually it's not,' he said, the hint of an accent evident once more in his deep, rich voice. He pointed to doors on the other side of the room that Holly had not even noticed. 'That's the way to the bathrooms. This is a communal lounge.'

'Oh.' She sat back down.

All is fine. He will continue through to the men's room. Then I can make a run for it.

But he did not leave.

After several uncomfortable moments, she glanced up to find him leaning casually against the far wall, blocking the way to the outer door, watching her.

His amused gaze scanned her dark hair piled high in a mass of controlled curls, past her face, which burned under his intent look, down her exposed neck and shoulders, making her wish she had a wrap to cover them.

As his regard skimmed lower she followed its direction and noticed that the length of her crossed legs was fully exposed through the split in her skirt. Sheathed in shimmering stockings, they glittered from toe to thigh, and the light scrape she had received from their scuffle on the footpath showed red through the filmy fabric. She uncrossed her legs, quickly swishing the soft cloth over them, hiding the wound.

The gesture was not lost on him and a fleeting, and utterly knee-melting, smile washed across his mouth, for a brief moment revealing overlapping front teeth and those unforgettable dimples.

Strength, Holly. Strength.

Her only glimmer of hope was that there had not been one hint of recognition in those laughing hazel eyes.

It was her. It had to be. She was the woman with the briefcase and the temper.

She was dressed so differently and not yelling at him—

Jacob ought not to have recognised her. But her gleaming dark hair, compelling blue eyes and natural elegance had meandered unbidden in and out of his mind so many times over the last day he had begun to think she had been no more than a jet-lag-induced delusion.

But she was real. And what a kick to walk through the door in search of a moment's peace and quiet only to find *her*, arranged before him like a delectable gift in such dazzling wrapping.

Jacob went to introduce himself. After all, they had met. Somewhat. And more to the point she could very well prove to be a delightful diversion during his hiatus here. Then he stopped himself.

She had recognised him too; it was splashed across her face, but she did not seem at all happy about it.

Sure, they had *clashed* rather than met, but that just made her all the more memorable. Yet instead of laughing it off or accusing him anew, she fussed and fidgeted and endeavoured to fade into the furniture. And despite her best efforts, that very bashfulness made her stand out like a luminous gem on her velvet cushion.

So maybe now was not the time to introduce himself. Maybe now was the time to enjoy watching her fuss and fidget some more.

'I know your face, but I can't seem to place you,' he said, staring at her as though sifting through his memory.

Help!

'Do you work for the company?' he asked.

Phew.

'No, thank heavens,' she said.

'You have something against Lincoln Holdings?'

She shrugged. 'I'm not a big fan of beer and boxing. So I guess that makes me not a big fan of Lincoln Holdings.'

He made no response, and seemed perfectly content in the long silence. On the contrary, Holly's right leg jiggled and her ears buzzed with every beat of her thudding heart.

'Are you planning on staying in here all night?' he finally asked.

'I hadn't really thought that far. I came with someone so I need the lift home.' She kept her eyes averted and her face turned as far away as was polite.

'I could organise a cab for you, if you wish.'

'No, thanks.' *Now off you go.*

'The least I can do is tell your companion you are in here,' the man said. 'I'm sure he would not want you out of his sight for too long.' And then he smiled again.

Holly felt like a whole family of butterflies had taken up residence in her stomach. It was unfair to have a debilitating smile like that in your arsenal. If he smiled at her like that one more time she would be reduced to a pile of quivering mush upon the fuzzy pink ottoman. It was maddening but she was drawn to him despite herself. So if he wasn't going to leave then she would have to.

'Maybe I should take a cab. Make Ben worry. He deserves it.'

'Ben?'

'I'm here with Ben Jeffries. One of the VPs.'

The man's attitude cooled so suddenly, it surprised Holly, then she remembered why she had embarked on her husband hunt in the first place. Her theory about the men she attracted. At parties.

He was no enigma, standing there seeming so cool and elegant. He had been wearing his party personality, he had been acting the part, just as they all did. He was good-looking enough to send a girl's stomach into a whole series of flips with one brief smile, and she had almost fallen for it.

The clang of a bell sounded from the other side of the door, followed by a loud cheer. Holly winced as she imagined the fighters coming together in a violent clash.

Her companion's attention focussed on her for one fleeting, intense moment, before he nodded, then headed back out into the throng.

The muffled sounds of the enthusiastic crowd outside infiltrated her conflicting thoughts. As she settled herself in for the duration it occurred to her that if it were not for that man's unpleasant behaviour at their first meeting, she would not have been sitting in a bathroom, dressed up, hungry and alone.

Smiling to herself, she felt much more comfortable thinking nothing but ill of him once more.

CHAPTER THREE

JACOB LINCOLN walked into his second-in-charge's office first thing Monday morning. He had been able to catch up for a brief hello and welcome home Saturday night but one subject had been bothering him since.

Without hesitation, Ben rounded his desk and hugged his old friend. He patted him on the back once more, as though making sure he was really there.

'I still can't believe you're back. And what an entrance. You sashayed into the match the other night, calm as you please, as if you'd never been away. Over the jet lag yet?'

'Pretty much. I had forgotten how cold and dry the air is in Melbourne. It hits you as soon as you get off the plane. I don't mind, though—I never could get used to the humidity in New Orleans.'

'Good. It means you're a Melbournian at heart.'

Jacob shrugged. 'Or maybe it means I should try San Francisco next.' Jacob sat down on the leather lounge chair on the near side of Ben's desk. His fingers unconsciously played with his bottom lip as he broached the subject that had been worrying him.

'At the fight, I met your date.'

Ben grinned broadly. 'So, you met the other woman in my life.'

Jacob's eyes narrowed at Ben's obvious affection towards a woman other than his pregnant wife. But Ben just burst out laughing.

'Don't look at me like that, Link. She's Beth's best friend. My poor wife can hardly walk up stairs any more, much less handle a nightclub function, so she asked me to take Holly. They've known each other for ever so when I fell madly in love with my wife, Holly came with the deal.'

Feeling undeniably better, Jacob leant back in the chair. 'What's she like?'

'You've met her. Short, blonde, heavily pregnant.' Ben reached for his wallet. 'I can show you a photo.'

'I meant Holly, and you know it.'

'Ah, Holly.' Ben put his wallet away.

'You get on well?' Jacob asked.

'You bet. So well, in fact, she has roped me into finding a man for her.'

'Really?' Surprising. She hardly seemed the type to need a blind date. But while he was in town…

'Not only a man,' Ben continued, shaking his head and smiling indulgently, 'but a husband at that.'

Whoa. A blind date was one thing…

He had been back in the country for just a few days and twice he had run into the same woman, and both times he had allowed her to get under his skin. He should have known better. So he swiftly latched onto the perfect balm for just that kind of irritant; she was on a husband hunt.

Suddenly San Francisco was looking better and better.

'She's cute, don't you think?' Ben asked with a glimmer in his eye.

'Sure.' If you called women with stormy blue eyes and legs that went on forever 'cute'.

'Did she happen to mention how she enjoyed the fight?'

'We met just before it began actually. But that didn't stop her pitching varied unflattering opinions about the match and my company in general.'

'That sounds like Holly. Did you…introduce yourself?' Ben asked, seeming to choose his words carefully. 'Did she know who you were?'

'She must have.' Jacob pictured her open book face and the recognition evident in every blink. 'What does that matter?'

'I guess it doesn't.'

Jacob stood and Ben walked him to the door.

'What are you doing for dinner tonight?' Ben asked. 'How does roast lamb grab you? Beth hasn't seen you for years and she would love to catch up before the baby's due.'

Though he had masses of work to do, the thought of such contented, uncomplicated company was too tempting to refuse.

'What time?'

'About seven?'

As Jacob left Ben's office he popped his head back in the door to say, 'By the way, I have never sashayed in my life.'

'It was horrible.' Holly was bent double with her bottom in the air and head pushed between her legs.

'Ben had a ball.' Beth did a far more gentle stretch with their yoga instructor watching her carefully.

'Of course he did. He's a man. And a Neanderthal at that, as I have only just discovered.'

'I promise if he'd told me beforehand it was that sort of function, I never would have suggested he take you. I'd told him a little about your dad, but not enough as it turned out.'

Beth laid a hand on Holly's arm. Holly shook it off, then instantly regretted the prickly move. She had long since let those memories lie and knew she was being overly sensitive.

'He thinks that Lincoln guy is "inspired",' Holly continued, her voice light. 'He has his head screwed on wrong.

If he really wanted his employees to bond in one of his establishments, why not buy a health resort and send them there? I could do a better job planning their parties half asleep and with one hand tied behind my back!'

'Or with your head between your knees, evidently.'

Holly flicked her friend a smile from between said knees.

'So, did you meet any honeys?' Beth asked.

'Nah,' Holly said, steadfastly failing to acknowledge the picture of sparkling hazel eyes that had fast formed in her mind. Besides, he was no honey. He was the enemy.

'I'm not surprised. May I ask how you hoped to find a husband in the "communal lounge"?'

'By that stage all I hoped to find was sanctuary from the rabble outside.'

'You would hardly want that to be the story you tell your grandkids. "We met on the way to the toilet…"'

'What's the point?' Holly sighed as she slowly stretched her arms to touch her toes. 'I will find no husband. I will have no grandkids to tell stories to.'

'Well, if that's your attitude I had better cancel your dinner date for tonight, then.'

'Dinner?' Holly stood up so fast she had to steady herself so as not to black out.

Beth stood more slowly and waddled over to their bags. Holly followed at a trot.

'To make up for his dismal effort the other night Ben has organised for one of his work colleagues to come to dinner tonight. He had hoped the two of you could meet, fall madly in love and marry. But if you're not interested—'

'Of course, I'm interested. Do you know him? Is he nice? Intelligent? What does he do? No, don't tell me. I don't want to know. Is he cute?'

'Just be at our place by six-thirty, and all will be revealed.'

'Yeah, yeah, yeah. Okay.' She gave Beth a big hug. 'You guys are so good to me.'

'Even Ben? A minute ago he was a Neanderthal.'

'Ben a Neanderthal? Never. He's the most wonderful man in the history of the world.'

Beth nodded, agreeing wholeheartedly.

As the clock neared seven Beth screamed at Ben to take Holly into the front room and keep her there. 'If she asks me what he's like one more time, the pair of you will be sucking gravy from your shirts.'

Holly took a seat in the front room. She crossed and uncrossed her legs several times before settling on right over left. She nibbled at her manicured fingernails and her right leg jiggled up and down.

A sudden downpour made a soft, rhythmic drumming sound on the flat roof. Holly watched as rain created hypnotic rivulets down the window-panes. Each car driving past was heralded by a soft swoosh of tyres on the wet road surface. Headlights lit up raindrops on the glass to a blinding brilliance, before fading as fast as they had arrived. But none heralded her blind date.

'Ben?'

'Yes, Holly.'

She knew that tone. Ben had already begun rubbing stiff fingers over the back of his neck.

'What does he know about me?'

'Are you sure you want to know? Are you sure you're not going to stop me as soon as I begin telling you?'

'I'm sure. Tell me. I can't stand it. I need to know something.' Holly's leg jiggled ever more violently.

'Okay,' he said. 'I told him that you were cute.'

'You said I'm cute?' Her leg jiggle slowed. 'You're so sweet.'

Ben mirrored her more relaxed behaviour. 'I told him that you and Beth had been friends for years—'

'He knows Beth well enough for you to mention I was friends with her?' she shrieked, and watched as a small muscle twitched in Ben's cheek. There was no stopping her. She was out of control.

'Maybe I should know who it is. No. I can't. Does Beth like him? What else did you tell him?'

Headlights flashed brightly through the window, though this time they shone directly through the lace curtains, and then switched off. Holly gulped as the engine sound stopped. He had arrived.

'I can't do this,' she whispered. 'Help.'

Ben stood and walked over to her, his jaw set. He grabbed her by the hand and pulled her to her feet. 'You want to know what else I told him about you?'

Ben propelled her to the front door. Holly knew that she had pushed him too far. She smiled in apology. 'I don't think I do.'

But it was too late. As the bell rang and just before Ben whipped open the front door he whispered in her ear.

'I told him you were on the prowl for a husband and he was candidate number one.'

CHAPTER FOUR

THE door swung open and Jacob found Holly frozen to the spot, her eyes wide and her mouth unnaturally ajar.

In that first moment, a broad smile swept across his face. He felt that same odd rush of warmth deep in the pit of his stomach that he felt each time he saw her.

Then he remembered Ben's revelation. The flowers he had brought for Beth drooped to his side. He glanced from Holly's curiously blanched face to Ben's apologetic one and he knew.

He had just turned up to a blind date with a husband hunter.

'Look, Holly. Flowers.' Ben grabbed the posy out of Jacob's hand and put them in Holly's, clasping her limp fist around the stems. 'Now, go put them in water.'

Ben spun her on the spot and gave her a little shove in the direction of the kitchen.

Jacob shrugged off his coat and shook his head to rid himself of a spray of raindrops that caught him on the way to the door, and then laid a friendly but controlling arm around his friend's shoulder. 'Is this what I think it is?'

'Mate, I'm sorry. I had a feeling neither of you would agree to come to dinner if I let on the other would be here.'

'You got that right.'

'If you are staying in town for any length of time you will be bound to run in the same circles so you may as well get to know each other.'

'Fair enough. But if that's all that this is, why is she acting like a living mummy?'

Ben flicked furtive glances towards the closed kitchen door. 'At times Holly can drive me around the bend, tonight being a prime example. And just before I opened the door I snapped and told her that—'

Ben stopped talking and swallowed. Jacob squeezed his friend's shoulder to hurry him up.

'I pretty much told her you knew she was "husband hunting" and that's why you were here.'

'You what?' Jacob dropped his arm from his friend's shoulder and took a step back, physically distancing himself from the shock.

'Look, Beth will be out any second, and she doesn't need too much excitement right now; so any shouting, and hitting, and telling Beth what I've done would create excitement. Please stay, eat a nice dinner. It'll all be over in a couple of hours.'

'I'll stay,' Jacob said through clenched teeth. 'For Beth.'

'Of course. And the shouting and hitting?'

'We'll save that for a rainy day.' Jacob grinned but it was all bared teeth and no pleasantry.

'And there's one more thing,' Ben said.

'What more could there possibly be?'

'It turns out Holly *doesn't* know you're Jacob Lincoln of Lincoln Holdings, which is a good thing as she really hated the whole boxing match and thus doesn't think much of him. You.'

Jacob blinked slowly. His mind was turning devilishly. Never one to shy away from a challenge—

'So, your Holly doesn't think much of me. Yet she thinks I have delivered myself here on a platter.'

'Yes. And?'

Jacob knew he had Ben worried. *Good.* 'Oh, I don't think you have the right to question me right now, my friend. No shouting, no hitting, now and for ever, as long as tonight you go along with whatever I throw at you. Deal?'

Ben looked over to the closed kitchen door. The water turned off and the kitchen door bumped as it started to open.

'Okay, deal,' Ben said.

Jacob slapped Ben on the back and grinned at his friend. But this time his smile was radiant with good humour.

Holly took her time fetching the food, and so gladly missed several minutes of chit-chat. That meant they were several minutes closer to the end of the night. Beth had just finished telling about the guitar lessons she was taking so she could play for her baby when Jacob informed the table at large that his younger sister was engaged.

'So that's why you're here,' Beth said. 'I knew it had to be more than just the temptation of my roast lamb. Have you met her fiancé?'

'I have. On Sunday. Nice guy,' Jacob said. 'This will be his second time around.'

'Divorced?' Beth asked.

'A widower.'

'Oh. Poor man. So he's older than Ana?'

'A good bit.'

'Doesn't surprise me, really, considering.' Beth brought her fingers to her temples and started to rub. 'Now, let me guess, knowing Ana, I bet he is in a caring profession. He's a...vet?'

'A triage nurse.'

Beth grinned. 'Oh, how perfect.'

'It would take someone with that sort of temperament to look after our Ana. She's quite a handful.'

'You would know.'

'No comment.'

Holly could tell there was some serious subtext to Beth's comments. She was intrigued despite herself, but her desire to stay invisible outweighed her curiosity so she let the conversation continue over her head.

'Anyway, good on him for taking her on,' Jacob said. 'I guess some people just like to be married.'

Holly stopped chewing and her cutlery stilled in her hand. *Did he seriously just say what I think he said?*

Ben coughed and she hoped he was choking on his potato. Beth's face, on the other hand, was all innocence. Perhaps Holly had misread the matter and Jacob was really talking about his sister, and not about her.

'Holly, could you please pass the broccoli?' Jacob asked.

Holly jumped in her seat at the call of her name. Her frazzled nerves were drawn as tight as Beth's new guitar strings. As she passed the bowl she locked eyes with the man across the table. He smiled bringing out his oh, so charming dimples.

He's the anti-husband, she reminded herself, *distant and indifferent. And his admittedly appealing dimples are, well, irrelevant.*

'Holly did the vegetables tonight, Jacob,' Beth said. 'She's a whiz with a steamer.'

Holly happily let go of the eye contact as she let go of the plate, and then shot Beth a quick yet entirely humourless smile.

'Anyway,' Jacob began again, 'Ana and Michael have known each other six months, been engaged for a week and are already talking kids.'

'Oh, that's wonderful,' Beth said.

'I'm all for short engagements,' Jacob said. 'She found someone like-minded, at the same point in his life, with the same goals and desires, and snapped him up. It was the smart thing to do.'

Was he serious? Holly had her reasons for embarking on her husband hunt, but what would Mr Standoffish be doing on a blind date with a woman he knew was after marriage? It made no sense. And, worse, it laughed in the face of her theory.

And who on earth was this guy? Ben had conveniently not let on what he did for the company. Maybe because Lincoln Holdings only kept him on in sympathy for some shocking flaw he hid under his cool good looks. Well, apart from the obvious personality defects Holly had already been subjected to.

To make matters worse, what if he eventually recognised her and let on that he was the guy on the street, the guy Beth knew had started her off on this crusade? If Beth knew, she would never let up about signs and primes and all sorts of gibberish. Holly was certain nothing bar that revelation could make this night more unbearable.

'I want kids, you know,' Jacob practically cooed. 'At least eight. No, eleven—a whole soccer team. So I should probably get started as soon as possible.'

Holly barely contained her groan. She lay down her cutlery, unable to stomach another bite.

Beth gave a painfully obvious nod towards Holly before asking, 'Do you have someone in mind to bear this football team for you?'

Holly glared ferociously at her friend, who refused to meet her eye.

'Not as such,' Jacob said, picking up a stem of broccoli on the end of his fork and twirling it before his eyes. 'But she would have to be a good cook. Though I would hope that she did not enjoy her own cooking so much that she not be able to keep her figure after the kids are born.'

What? Was this guy for real?

Jacob had trouble keeping the smile from his voice. Ben had his head buried in his hands, Beth's eyes were widening in shock with each absurd statement, and the lovely Holly was slumping lower and lower in her chair.

'Ben and I talked about this today. Didn't we, Ben?' Jacob casually cracked a knuckle or two as if to say, *Your choice: shouting and hitting or go with the flow.* Ben smiled ruefully and nodded.

'Constantly, mate. Hardly got any work done, we were so busy talking about kids.'

But Jacob wasn't finished yet—

'And I do like blondes. If I were to marry a brunette I would ask that she dye her hair. I mean, if she really cared for *my* feelings she would do that, wouldn't you think?'

Jacob revelled in the stunned silence that met his latest words. *Got 'em!*

'So, Holly, how about you?'

'Excuse me?' Holly squeaked.

'How many kids do you want?' Jacob asked.

Holly darted a hunted gaze to her friends but found no help from their corner. Ben was finding his cutlery very interesting whilst Beth still stared at Jacob, her eyes bright with astonishment.

'Umm…kids?' she said. 'I haven't really thought about it.'

'No? I'm surprised at that.'

'Surprised?' Her voice was still an octave too high and barely above a whisper. She cleared her throat.

'Don't all women think of these things? How many and what you would name them all?'

'I guess,' Holly admitted whilst wishing she could dissolve into the floor.

'And haven't you had a distinct idea of the man you would one day marry?'

And then he smiled. From ear to ear. Adorably overlapping teeth, charming dimples and enough charisma to knock her socks off. If he had held up a big sign with an arrow pointing to himself it would not have been more obvious. He seemed so ripe he probably kept his grandmother's ring in the top pocket of his jacket every day…just in case.

She swallowed hard. Her brow was furrowed so tight it was giving her a headache. She knew her terrible poker face would be showing all the signs of the strain she felt. She could feel hot red blotches forming on her neck and cheeks. But she had no idea how to extricate herself from this nightmare.

Then suddenly Jacob's bright eyes narrowed, seemingly looking deeper and deeper into her own until she was sure she saw a softening. A melting. The impenetrable myriad hazel flecks in his gaze grew deep and kind and sad. For a flicker she sensed an apology, as real as if he had said it aloud.

And although she would have thought it impossible, it made her knees feel weaker than they had all night.

He had done enough. He had proven his point. After this performance, Ben and Beth would not dare to set him up on this kind of date again. And that was all he wanted from the night. So he changed tack.

'How about you, Beth? Did you think you'd end up with someone soft and fuzzy like young Benny boy?'

As Beth proceeded to regale the group with tales of

numerous dream boys from her teens Jacob watched as Holly slowly relaxed.

Her natural colour had returned and he noticed again what an attractive woman she was—and just his taste. Not too tall, graceful, curvaceous, vivacious. And he had been lying earlier to rile her. He had never been one of those men who preferred blondes. Her lustrous, thick dark hair beguiled him. He found himself wanting to release it from its confining pins and feel its lush abundance sliding through his fingers.

With her head cocked, listening to Beth's funny stories, she surreptitiously picked up stray slivers of carrot and brought them to her mouth, daintily sucking them in with a swift sip. And each time she gave the tips of her fingers an unhurried lick, savouring the slight drops of honey. And Jacob was mesmerized. It was all he could do to stop himself from licking his own lips, she made it look so good.

'Don't you remember Gary Phelps, Holly?' Beth asked, snapping Jacob back to the conversation at hand. Holly even managed a small laugh. It was a pretty sound. Light and unselfconscious.

'He was so horrid, Beth.' Holly grimaced, but her voice had returned to a more normal timbre.

'He was not. He was lovely.'

'He was five feet tall and never washed his hair. I never knew what you saw in him.'

'Just because he wasn't tall, dark and handsome like every boy you ever had a crush on didn't mean he couldn't be attractive to someone else. Namely me. And what a kisser.'

Holly flicked a sudden glance Jacob's way. If he had blinked, he would have missed it, but he had caught its full measure. It was a look brimming with suppressed attraction. He should have jumped from his seat and run for his life. But he didn't.

She had bruised his ego enough with her indifference towards his business practices. So he intended to soak up every bit of positive attention she was willing to send his way. Just to even the scales. That was all.

'Hey,' Ben called out, feigning a broken heart. 'You do realise your husband and the father of your soon to be child is sitting here having to listen to these stories of young love which do not involve him.'

'Yes, darling but you have to remember that, out of this long line of dreamboats, I chose you.'

'Very true.' Ben beamed lovingly at his wife.

Under the mask of laughing along with them, Jacob stole a cheerful glance over Holly, and he found her leaning her chin on her palm, watching Ben and Beth with a smile of pure joy splashed across her lovely face. Her expression was so tender it was luminous. And in that moment he thought he understood her. It did not seem so very strange to want what Ben and Beth had.

Jacob felt a sudden tightening in his chest. Not good. He needed time out. He pushed his chair back and stood up.

'Excuse me, folks. I have to powder my nose.'

As soon as Jacob left Beth leaned forward and whispered conspiratorially, 'What on earth is with him tonight, Ben? All that talk of babies and blondes, that wasn't like the Jacob Lincoln of old.'

'*Lincoln?*' Holly mimicked Beth's strained whisper, as it was the only way she could stop herself from shouting. '*He's* Jacob Lincoln? As in your boss, Link? As in Lincoln Holdings *Lincoln*?'

Ben flinched. 'Ah, yes. He's one and the same.'

'What on earth is he doing here? You told me he lived in…New Orleans or some such place.' And he was supposed to be balding, with a paunch and liver spots. Not…well, not so manifestly the opposite.

'He did,' Ben said. 'Then without telling a soul he moved back to Melbourne a couple of days ago.'

That first morning, standing on the corner, armfuls of luggage, faint accent. Holly dropped her face into her palms.

'That means I told him how little I thought of his boxing idea, not at the time realising that it was his idea, then accused him of going to the wrong bathroom, not at the time realising it was his bathroom. He's really Jacob *Lincoln*?' she repeated.

Ben shrugged and grinned contritely.

Holly's voice hissed as she turned on Ben, her pent-up mortification whirling into a terrible rage. 'And knowing all of this you set up this dinner, told him that I was "husband hunting", and that he was my number one contender?'

Beth also turned on her husband. 'Did you really do all of those things?'

Ben held his hands up in submission. 'Hey, you guys dragged me into this ridiculous plan of yours. So, I took you to a gathering teeming with numerous available red-blooded men and you hid in the bathroom all night. And then I ask the most eligible of all red-blooded men I know to dinner and you attack me.'

Holly was having none of it. 'But you told him—'

'The truth, Holly. But to tell *you* the truth I really did wonder if my two best friends in the whole world might not hit it off.'

Beth's face softened easily. 'That's so sweet. Holly, forgive Ben.'

Holly sat back, all angered out. Her face was heated from her strained whispers and her head spun with the maze of words and deeds they had created for themselves.

Beth giggled. 'Now poor Jacob thinks Holly's hot for him. No wonder he has been acting so strangely.'

'Ah, well, actually,' Ben said, 'he knows the whole deal and has been pulling your legs all night.'

'Ha!' Beth said, clapping her hands together. 'Now that's more like the Jacob Lincoln of old.'

But Holly was not so amused. She was thinking. And planning. 'He knows the whole deal and he thinks I'm now sweating it.'

'Well, gorgeous, you have pretty much been sweating it all night,' Ben said.

'But I'm not now.' Now she knew the glimmer in Jacob's eyes had indicated he was enjoying an elaborate joke, not that he was sizing her up for a wedding dress.

Well, if it was fun and games he liked...

CHAPTER FIVE

WHEN Jacob re-entered the room Holly was standing by her empty chair, eyes closed, rocking her head side to side. He suppressed a grin as he settled back in his chair. He shouldn't have been worried; he still had the upper hand. He had the poor woman in knots.

As he watched she ran a hand up her side, and then back and forth across her shoulder, eyes still closed, head tossed back, leisurely massaging out those very knots. Her mouth dropped open and a blissful groan escaped her lips.

Whoa.

Jacob shifted in his seat, suddenly feeling mighty uncomfortable. He set his teeth and tore his eyes away before he would be forced to make another hasty exit to recollect his wits.

'What did I miss?' he asked, purposely not including Holly in his question.

But Holly had ceased her rub-down, and Jacob's gaze was magnetically drawn to the movement. He did not miss a single curve as her hand made its unhurried journey back down her side to rest provocatively on her hip.

'Nothing significant, Jacob,' Holly purred. 'I was just saying how much I was hankering for something sweet.'

Her lashes batted heavily against her cheeks, then her gaze fluttered and drifted to his lips.

The words 'then come and get it' sat precariously close to the tip of Jacob's tongue. *Get a hold of yourself,* he told himself. *You're imagining things. You're just tired. It's not been a week; can you still blame the jet lag?*

'Time for dessert, then, I think,' Beth said, her voice cheerful. Jacob flicked his glance to his other dinner companions. He had momentarily forgotten they were even there.

It took all of Jacob's concentration to focus on Beth, chatting to her about her nursery plans, resolutely ignoring Holly as she moved around the table clearing the dinner plates. His resolve weakened as he sensed her reach the back of his chair and it shattered when she bent to retrieve his plate and fanned a warm breath of air against his ear. It was all he could do to keep a straight face as a violent shiver racked his body.

Then, before disappearing into the kitchen, Holly turned and threw him a sultry wink.

Jacob stared at the closed kitchen door. She had assured him nothing significant had happened in his absence. She had fibbed.

In five mystery minutes, she had transformed from an overwhelmed young woman into a raging siren. And despite himself he was enthralled. Under that haughty façade lurked a hell-cat just waiting to claw her way out. It could be a lot of fun unlocking the door to that particular cage.

Jacob blinked his eyes back into focus to find Ben red-faced and shaking with laughter and Beth wiping tears of mirth from her cheeks.

And the truth dawned on him.

'She knows.' Jacob threw his napkin on the table in defeat.

'She knows,' Ben admitted. 'Shouting and hitting from you is nothing compared with the combined wrath of those two.'

'So,' Beth asked, her voice playful, 'are you going to propose to her now or after dessert?'

*   *   *

From the kitchen, Holly was glad to hear laughter.

She was about to return to the dining room to retrieve the cutlery when the kitchen door flapped open and Jacob joined her, cutlery in hand.

'Oh.' She took a step back, swamped by the man's considerable presence in the small kitchen. He leant past her to place the silverware in the sink, the sleeve of his dark grey suit jacket brushing against her arm. The sensation of the roughened wool against smooth bare skin was electric.

'I'm happy to clear. Go sit back down.' She waved him away with a flourish, and took two steps back leaving her flush against the kitchen cupboards. She desperately hoped he would leave her alone. But hoping did not make it so.

'Actually, I'm here to talk. The cutlery was just an excuse.'

'Oh,' she murmured again.

'That was some act you put on in there.'

Her blush was back. 'Your performance wasn't so bad either.'

He lowered his voice so that it washed over her as a soft rumble. 'Though I don't know that I can outdo your last turn—not with an audience, anyway.'

Gulp.

'So how about we call it even?' He held out his hand. 'Truce?'

Holly stared for several moments before reaching out and clasping it. His hand was soft and strong and she was thankful his palm was as warm as hers. When she let go she ran a nervous finger around the neckline of her dress.

'And I also wanted to apologise for that morning on the street.'

Holly's finger stopped, mid tug.

'That was atypical behaviour for me,' he said. 'And

though I *was* jet-lagged, that was no excuse for bad manners.'

He stopped talking and Holly realised he was waiting for her to say something next.

'You didn't tell Ben that, did you?' she blurted out. Or Ben would have told Beth for sure and there would be no living it down. 'You didn't let on we had met before? That we met that way?'

'Ah, not as far as I remember.'

'Then don't. Please. For reasons inexplicable and uninteresting I would rather our first meeting stay our little secret.'

'Sure.'

Holly blinked. She had expected it to be harder than that. According to her theory he was supposed to be obstinate and unyielding.

'And one more thing, just to clear the air,' Jacob said.

'Go for your life.' So glad she was safe from Beth's karma and kismet conversation, Holly was ready to tell him anything.

'Do you mind telling me why you think you need Ben's help to find a husband?' He leant his large frame against the cupboards at her side and she had to look up to meet his eye.

'Oh,' she said for the third time in as many minutes, the blush now spreading all the way to her toes. 'Isn't that a little personal?'

Jacob laughed. 'Personal? You were ready to marry me before seven o'clock tonight.'

Holly's hands flew from where they gripped the cool kitchen sink to cover her fast-reddening cheeks. 'Don't remind me, please.'

She slowly lowered her hands from her face, thinking it

must have been hot in the small room. His cheeks were as pink as hers felt. She wasn't just imagining it.

Then without warning Jacob raised his hand and ran a finger over a stray lock of hair that had escaped its confines. He slid it back into place behind her ear, his fingertip resting by her cheek for a few lingering moments. And during those long drawn-out seconds she could not have dragged her eyes away from his for all the world.

The scraping of a chair in the dining room brought Holly out of her reverie and she spun around to face the plates of dessert she had been preparing. Jacob cleared his throat and walked from the room without another word.

Holly went to pick up two plates and saw that her hands were shaking. She carefully placed the plates back onto the bench and took a couple of deep breaths.

'He's the enemy, remember,' she said aloud. 'The anti-husband. He was put on this earth to test you. If you can resist him, you can resist any of his kind.' She glared at her hands, demanding they not shake as she took the plates into the other room.

Hours later Holly helped Beth up to the master bedroom and left the men to say their goodnights downstairs. As Beth got into bed she said, 'He's a sweetie, Holly.'

'Of course he is or you wouldn't have married him.'

'I mean Jacob, you dope.'

Sweet's the last word I'd use, Holly thought. 'Yeah, well, the jury is still out on that one.'

'Promise me you'll give him a chance.'

Not likely. 'Sure, honey. For you, anything.'

'Good…goodnight…'

Holly kissed her sleepy friend on the cheek and headed quietly downstairs. The men's voices wafted up the stairwell. Holly stopped halfway down, her heart beating so loudly in her ears she was sure they would hear it too and know she was there.

'Give her a chance,' she heard Ben say. It made her smile, thinking how alike Ben and Beth were. But her smile soon faded at Jacob's response.

'Give me a break, Ben, I've been back in the country for a few days, and haven't even found the time to acquire a housekeeper. Besides which I have no idea how long I'm staying this time *and* you know my views on marriage. What were you thinking?'

She knew it! In that first instant when they had crashed together on the street she had seen it. She sensed this guy was the epitome of the inaccessible male. He was the antithesis of kind, committed Ben. Her theory had been right all along.

Holly strained to listen when there was a brief pause in the conversation.

'Unless of course she's handy with a feather duster… then both of our problems would be solved in one fell swoop.'

Charming! She waited for Ben's protest—which never came.

'Not likely, I'm afraid. A bit of a princess, our Holly.'

Ben! He always joked she would not know one end of a broom from the other, but did he have to describe her that way to a stranger? She pictured him describing her to other prospective men. 'She's a cutie, our Holly,' she could imagine Ben saying. 'She can cook up a storm but it will be you scrubbing the bathroom tiles.'

Great. No wonder his first attempts had been such failures. Well, she would sort him out later so they could get this project back onto track.

Holly made great noise coming down the rest of the stairs, clumping loudly and whistling inanely.

'Isn't Beth asleep?' Ben asked, shushing her.

Holly clenched her fists at her side. 'Thanks for a *super* evening, Benny,' she said.

Jacob helped her into her coat at the front door. She wrapped a scarf around her neck but held onto her gloves, glaring at Ben and mouthing unpleasant promises as he waved goodbye and closed the front door with a soft click.

The rain had stopped but had left a slick sheen on the ground so Holly had no choice but to accept Jacob's elbow as they walked down the slippery front steps.

At the bottom of the driveway they reached Holly's car and she finally jerked her arm away. 'Thank you,' she said. Her breath showed white in the frosty midnight air.

'My pleasure.' He slipped his hands into his deep pockets.

'Look—' They both spoke at the same time. Jacob motioned for Holly to speak first.

'It's unlikely we will run into each other often, so, I think it best we just pretend we never met.'

'Sure,' Jacob said. 'No problem.'

Hmm. She had expected, 'If you say so,' or even, 'If you insist.' But, 'No problem'? Was she that easily forgettable?

Bothered beyond good sense, she mustered her haughtiest attitude. 'No matter what Ben told you, and not that it matters what you think, I am no princess.'

Jacob laughed, his head thrown back as he let out great effusive guffaws. Holly was shocked into momentary silence.

'You heard that?' Jacob finally asked, his eyes sparkling in merriment.

'Loud and clear. And I think that was extremely wrong of Ben and rude of you to even joke about such a thing.'

'Are you done?'

She looked up, surprised at his short tone.

'Well, yes, I thought that quite about covered it—'

Jacob leant over and placed a light kiss on her open mouth, succeeding in shutting her up. His hands remained in his pockets and her hands held her gloves in front of her at chest height. And since his toes were a couple of feet from hers, the only points of contact were their four, warm, amenable lips.

It took the merest moment for the unexpected tenderness of his kiss to wash its magic over her. On impulse Holly closed her eyes and tilted her head only ever so slightly. But it was enough.

Jacob took her hint and he leant that little bit closer to explore the warmth and thrill as unexpected yearning lit between them. And what started as little more than an overly friendly goodnight peck deepened into something very different. It was delicate. It was yielding. It was lovely.

After enjoying a few moments of unchecked ardour, they pulled apart.

Holly rocked back on her heels; luckily the car was there to catch her as she swayed. Her tongue ran over the back of her teeth and she could taste after dinner mints. She rocked forward as she opened her eyes and sighed, unconsciously biting her lower lip.

The adorable dimples reappeared on Jacob's smooth cheeks as he smiled. 'I think now it's time to go our separate ways. You and I have already created far too many inconsistent memories for one night.'

'Goodnight, Jacob,' Holly whispered, not trusting her husky voice.

'Goodnight, Holly,' he said, but his eyes were saying anything but. He let out a ragged breath, shook his head and turned away.

Holly dragged in a deep breath, revelling in the sweet smell of recent rain that wafted towards her on the light night breeze.

She opened her car door but turned quickly when she saw him coming back up the rise. She leant back on her car, holding her breath waiting to see what he would surprise her with next.

'I have to say this,' he declared, his face obscured by the darkness. 'You are an intriguing, vibrant and beautiful woman, Holly. Know your own worth.'

And then he turned and disappeared into the foggy night.

CHAPTER SIX

HOLLY waited until in between races to make her way from the big white marquee on the oval in the centre of the track where the Hidden Valley Greyhound Course fundraiser was being held. She stepped carefully, lifting her feet high as she made her way across the muddy dirt track.

Colonel Charles Lyneham, a long-retired Steward of the Course and her guest of honour, had gone for a walk around an hour before and had not returned, so Holly had set out to find him.

She ducked through a spot in the fence where the wire had broken away years before and headed up the old wooden steps to the grandstand. She checked in the clerk's offices, the betting areas and even in the car park. But the colonel was nowhere to be seen. She headed for the public bar, hoping she would not find him there.

As she rounded the corner the scene hit her like *déjà vu*. The smell of beer, mud and sweat. She, standing on the outside looking in, searching for someone she had lost. The only difference was years before her view had been from a couple of feet closer to the ground. At least now she was the right height to have a chance at finding a familiar silver-topped head standing tall above the pack.

She lifted on tiptoe but instead of finding said familiar silver-topped head, she recognised a pair of stunning, laughing hazel eyes looking her way.

Her heels dropped straight to the ground, her mind turning to the last time she had seen those eyes; midnight in a fog-shrouded street, after an exquisite kiss that had confused her exceedingly.

Suddenly a man reached out from the throng and grabbed her by the elbow, drawing her within the swelling crowd and giving her a big brotherly kiss on the cheek.

'Ben! What are you doing here?' Holly said, looking behind him half expecting Jacob to be hot on his trail.

'The company has a corporate box and Link sequestered it for the day. All the management guys are here for a welcome home bash. Come join us.'

'I can't, Ben. I'm here on a mission not a play date.' She tried to step back outside the bar but the crowd had long since swallowed them whole. 'Have you seen Charles Lyneham? He's with my party and seems to have gone walkabout.'

'The colonel? He's with us.'

Ben held her fast by the arm and dragged her through the crush. Bumped and jostled from all sides, she had no choice but to hug Ben's arm with both hands and hang on tight.

'Link found him wandering around outside after the first race,' Ben said. 'He coaxed him in for a tipple and he's been with us ever since. Now you'll have to come say hello.'

'Great,' Holly said. 'He's due to make a thank-you speech at our fundraiser in little under half an hour, and, the thing is, Charlie does not merely *tipple*. Now, thanks to your friend, if he's been in the bar *tippling* for an hour, it's very likely he will be there all day.'

Ben shrugged but had the good grace to look sheepish. 'Sorry, gorgeous.'

Jacob's hearty laughter rang out above their conversation and, despite her deliberate disapproval, she enjoyed every second of the delightful sound, an unwitting smile tugging at the corners of her own mouth. He certainly cut a compelling picture, standing taller than most of the others, one hand wrapped around a frosty glass of beer, the other tucked into the pocket of his suit trousers, and one foot casually resting on the bottom rung of a bar stool.

He was just ten feet away. The room was airless and muggy. Her face was hot and her palms sweating. And with each step nearer her heartbeat quickened.

She tottered after Ben, still holding tight so she wouldn't tumble and be crushed underfoot. She ventured a furtive glance around. No sign of Charlie, but she had no doubt he would not be far away.

Five feet. She felt eager and sick to the stomach all at once.

Come on, look up, see me. Let's just get it over with. Let's see if that kiss meant as little to you as it did to me.

'Link,' Ben called out over the noise.

Jacob looked their way. His ready smile brightened, and he winked as he caught sight of Ben. Then his glance shifted sideways to Holly and the smile changed.

His bright eyes darkened, clouded, his thick lashes descended mere millimetres until he was watching her from beneath them. The corners of his mouth fell. The warmth in his expression was more than a match for the heat pulsing through her body at that moment.

Then his gaze left her face to glance down to where she was hugging Ben's left arm tight to her chest.

She let go. Quickly. Hating the fact she must have seemed so helpless, in her neat dress, her prim hair, clinging to Ben for protection against the unruly crowd.

Ben did not seem to notice, he just turned and smiled and placed a protective arm behind her back as he drew her into the group.

When Jacob looked back to Holly's face his smile was

gone, and his once warm eyes were now cool and unreadable. He brought his glass up, and tilted it in her direction in an abrupt salute before drinking in a substantial mouthful and turning back to his men.

Holly's face burned. Sure, she had been the one to insist they pretend they had never met, but, still, she had not expected it to be so easy for him. In his company she could feel her pulse throbbing all the way to her toes. Yet this guy obviously felt nothing. He was too cool.

Ugh! Why had she expected it to be any different? She *knew* she had him pegged but for a moment had foolishly expected him to prove her wrong. Well, it looked as if her theory still stood the test. So be it.

She deliberately turned away from Jacob and assumed her most brilliant smile.

'I heard you gentlemen had waylaid a friend of mine.'

The men stopped talking as one.

'Sorry, Holly,' Ben said, 'it slipped my mind. Holly is in charge of the fundraiser under the big marquee and it seems we have stolen away her guest of honour.' He looked around, his hand never leaving Holly's back. 'Where has the young colonel gone?'

'It's his round, I'm afraid,' one young, good-looking member of the group said, his eyes on Holly, full of invitation. 'No way we could let him go until he'd paid his debt. So, you'll just have to wait with us until he gets back. And since this great lug won't introduce us, I'm Matt Riley. The new Accounts guy.'

'Nice to meet you Matt. I'm Holly Denison.' She shook his hand. It held hers for a fraction longer than necessary.

'I know,' he said.

Ben's joke came swimming back to her and Holly had visions of her photograph and phone number in the men's room at his work—

'I saw you at the fight.'

This guy was at the fight? He was one of the men she'd had the possibility of meeting that night? She took a closer look at the very real option before her. Tall, athletic, nice smile. Very cute.

Then from behind her Jacob openly scoffed. Holly spun on her heel and turned narrowed eyes his way, but to little avail. His distant expression was unaltered.

'You must have good eyesight, Riley. She was there for all of ten seconds.'

His gaze held hers without a hint of remorse. She glared back, her infuriated eyes daring him to go on and at the same time demanding he say not another word.

He turned to face Matt and shrugged. 'From what Benny boy told me, anyway.'

'Well, obviously ten seconds was enough to make an impression on me. But you did your runner before I had the chance to say hi.'

Holly spun back to face her new suitor and beamed, before flicking a smug grin over her shoulder at Jacob.

'You don't say.'

Go, Matt, she thought, *you're definitely younger, possibly cuter, and certainly more of a gentleman than the loud mouth behind me. Fair where Jacob is dark. Candid where Jacob is confusing. Yes, very cute indeed. But I think you know it too. Highly likely* another *party personality at work.*

Suddenly disinclined to play favourites, she broke away from Matt's concentrated attention and introduced herself to several other young men, most of them her age, a couple of them uncommonly good-looking. These guys were in the inner sanctum so they were obviously smart, successful and hand picked by Ben to work at Lincoln Holdings. This was exactly who Ben should have been setting her up with.

She was able to enjoy the possibilities for several moments until she once more locked eyes with Jacob. He wasn't smiling at her as the other men were; he was practically smirking. Sitting back, arms crossed, like an omniscient little devil watching over her. Evidently, he knew exactly what was going on in her mind.

Holly plastered the smile to her face and shrugged. Why deny it? What was it to him anyway?

'Holly, my sweet. How good of you to join us.' It was the colonel, back with a round of drinks. 'I would have invited you to come up here with me but it's been years since I have seen you step foot in this ancient inn.'

'Charlie,' Holly said, her antagonism subsiding in the company of the darling old man, 'you know I would go anywhere you asked me to. But we do have another arrangement today. Remember the fundraiser?'

Charlie nodded.

'The big marquee? Your thank-you speech?'

He stopped nodding. 'Oh.'

She studied him carefully for signs he had been drinking. He was sweating a little, but so was she in the hot, confined space. He was upright and his speech was not slurred. Shy of sniffing the drink in his hand she had no idea if he had been 'tippling' as Ben had suggested.

'I suggest we let Charlie finish his *lemonade*,' Jacob said, 'then we can all head down and listen to this great speech of his. What do you say, Ms Denison?'

Lemonade? Holly looked up into Jacob's face in amazement. Gone was the smirk. In its stead was a raised eyebrow, an easy smile. *How had he known?*

'Sounds fair to me,' Holly said, sending Jacob a terse nod of thanks.

The colonel downed the remainder of his lemonade with one swift, practised flick of his wrist. 'Off we go then.'

Holly turned towards the front of the bar and found she was confronted once more by a seething mass of white shirts and ties. She physically dreaded forcing her way through the hot, sweaty throng. But then Jacob's voice bellowed from just behind her.

'Clear the way, gentlemen! The colonel is coming through.'

All of the men nearby acquiesced, and once the Chinese whispers spread through the place a clear, snaking path, an amazing sort of honour guard, formed from their table to the door. The colonel smoothed down his suit and with head held high traversed the way.

Holly felt a warm hand land softly in the small of her back. She turned to find Jacob bowing gallantly towards her, his face mere inches from her own.

'Shall we, Ms Denison?' He removed his warm hand and offered his elbow. She looked into his quixotic hazel eyes searching for a trap. Unfortunately they were as inscrutable as he chose them to be.

Ahead of her the extraordinary meandering path was threatening to collapse back in on itself. For once Jacob's company seemed the lesser of two evils, so she took his arm and walked at his side.

The back of Holly's hand rubbed against Jacob's shirt-covered bicep, the sensation heated, intoxicating, reprehensible. Thankfully the awareness of that tantalising touch was short-lived, as soon the peripheral heat was all that registered.

The room was stifling, her view filled with sweaty, leering faces. Somebody trod on her foot and spinning around to apologise, they spilt drink down her side. She leapt back, clutching onto Jacob's arm with both hands. He immediately wrapped a protective hand over the top of hers, its warmth and tenderness calming her a little.

Feeling claustrophobic, she closed her eyes, and allowed herself to be led the rest of the way blind. Only once bright sunlight lit the inside of her eyelids blood red did she open them.

Finding they were now in the big open space at the top of the grandstand, she hungrily inhaled the fresh, cool winter air, her breath releasing on a shudder.

She turned to thank Jacob but he was in conversation with two of his men, pointing towards the track where Race Three had just begun. And Holly knew she would not get any sense from any of them until the event was over.

The first two races had been won by the favourites and Holly expected no different ending to this one. She remained silent, unmoved as the dogs rounded the final bend.

The sparse crowd in the grandstand rose to its collective feet and the men in her own party jumped up and down, yelling and screaming, and clutching their betting slips in tight, agitated fists. The favourite, Sir Pete, was a nose behind, and the possibility of an upset electrified the air.

'I don't know why they get so excited,' Holly muttered under her breath, 'Sir Pete will win.'

'Don't bet on it,' Jacob said equally quietly, his eyes bright.

'I never would.'

Then, in the last twenty metres, Sir Pete put on a phenomenal burst of speed and finished two body lengths ahead of his nearest competitor.

'I hate to lose,' Jacob said through comically clenched teeth as he ceremoniously tore up his losing bet.

'So pick the favourite.'

A huge grin broke out over his face, its effortless bril-

liance surprising her, catching her unawares and sending a
blissful rush from her neck to her toes.

'You are one surprising woman, Holly Denison.'

Definitely time to go back to her party.

CHAPTER SEVEN

ONLY when Holly made to follow her departing group did she find herself still attached to Jacob's arm. Flicking him an apologetic smile, she released her steel grip. But he pulled her back until she was flush against him.

'Not just yet, Ms Denison. Before I let you go, I have a question I simply must have answered.'

His voice was low and husky. His face was in shadow, and his dark hair in a halo of sunlight as he stood with his back to the sun.

'Ask away,' she said, her voice reedy.

'What on earth are you wearing on your feet?'

Holly blinked. Looked at her feet. And grinned. In all the confusion, she had plum forgotten.

'Haven't you even seen a pair of galoshes before, Mr Lincoln?'

'Of course. I have even seen ones that yellow before. But not, I must admit, on a grown woman, otherwise dressed to the hilt as you are. Is this some kind of fashion statement?'

'Hmm. You have been away too long, haven't you? Bright yellow galoshes are Melbourne's must-have fashion item this winter.'

'Throw out the little black dress?' he asked.

Holly brought her spare hand to her heart and gasped in mock shock. 'Gosh, no. Never. But wear with the little black dress? Of course.'

Jacob nodded, his expression deadly serious, as though

impressed by her wealth of fashion knowledge. He eased her into a slow ramble towards the grandstand steps.

'Now you've answered the what, do I get to hear the why?'

Holly paused a moment for effect. 'So my feet don't get wet.'

Jacob glanced at her sideways and raised one unconvinced eyebrow.

'Okay. After last night's downpour, I arrived this morning to find the ground below my marquee ankle-deep in mud. Rather than have guests whose only memory of the day would be their wet feet, and without having to move the whole shebang up to a dreary old conference room with no view of the track, I brought in enough galoshes and warm socks to shoe my entire guest list.'

As her tale unfurled Jacob stopped watching the group ahead of him, and concentrated fully on her, his eyes growing bright with delight.

'And besides you, did *anybody* actually dare to wear them?'

'Sure. Everybody.'

Holly pulled Jacob up short as they had reached the fence line that separated the crowd from the track. Jacob looked about for the rest of their group and finding them heaving themselves awkwardly over the fence several metres away, he tried tugging her in their direction.

But Holly tugged him back.

She beamed at him proudly, then slipped effortlessly through the concealed hole in the fence that the others did not know was there. Jacob watched in amazement before following her through.

They trudged across the muddy dirt track, nearing the huge white marquee, which glowed brightly in the midday sun, the canvas roof flapping softly in the light breeze. The sounds of clinking glasses and happy chatter wafted across the way.

Holly smiled inwardly. Jacob looked so dubious. His expression was like a child's on Christmas Day, just before opening his present from Grandma. Would it be the monster truck he had been promised or would it be tartan hankies again?

Jacob's doubt was written so clearly across his face that Holly's inward smile twisted with sadness. She had the feeling that he probably always doubted good things could happen until he saw them with his own two eyes. This was a man who knew disappointment.

The men ahead of them lifted the flap and headed inside. Holly and Jacob came close on their heels. Enjoying the moment intensely, Holly made sure she got there first. She grabbed a hold of the big flap and feeling like a ringmaster, opened it with a flourish.

Jacob was astounded.

Inside the marquee were glass-topped tables, candlelight shimmered from every spare surface and even from makeshift chandeliers hanging low from the ceiling. Heaters were scattered discreetly throughout the tent. The walls crawled with ivy interweaved with daisies and daffodils. The effect was like a mirage, a dash of springtime in the middle of the gloomy, muddy oval outside.

He scanned the faces of the people in the room. Many familiar, several famous. All laughing and drinking and obviously having a ball. And all were wearing bright yellow galoshes.

He turned to Holly, who was watching him with a satisfied grin splashed across her lovely face.

'I am impressed.'

'And your feet?' she asked.

Jacob lifted one foot and saw the kid leather was wet through and through. 'Ruined. Even my socks are soaked.'

Holly gave a quick nod to someone outside Jacob's field of view and within a couple of seconds a waiter arrived, the tray in his arms laden with a pair of brand new galoshes and a pair of thick cotton socks, both in size extra large.

'Do I have to?' he asked.

'What do you think?'

In answer Jacob grabbed the galoshes and pulled up a spare garden chair. He held up his wet leather lace-ups and the waiter swapped the ruined shoes for a cloakroom ticket and disappeared to look after other guests.

'There,' Holly said. 'Now you fit in. Now you're one of us.'

She turned away to give instructions to an earnest young man with a clipboard. She was efficient. She liked being in control.

And then he realised: she was happy because he had done what *she* wanted him to do. He bristled, hating the feeling of being constrained, of being dared to make a choice not his own.

He was a free man with nothing and no one holding him down. He had lived that other life, being beholden to someone else's needs and wishes. And he never wanted to go that way again. Then he stopped himself.

Relax. It's a pair of shoes. This is one afternoon. You can give over to someone else's wishes for one afternoon. It's not like you will be giving over the decision-making to the woman for a lifetime.

A lifetime. And he remembered. She was on the hunt for a husband and had convinced Ben to help her.

Why? She was gorgeous. Slim, with curves in all the right places and the sort of lush dark hair any man would

love to run his fingers through. And he knew those legs
of hers were long, lithe, and smooth, though right now half
hidden beneath those ridiculous rubber boots.

She had been attracting plenty of interested looks since
she had walked in, and earlier his men had practically
tripped over each other for the sake of one of her smiles.

Jacob observed a couple of well-dressed sorts on the
other side of the tent obviously talking about her. And he
felt an unexpected urge to go to her. To shield her from
their view. To defend her against their scrutiny.

She must have caught him watching her as she raised
her eyebrows in question. She held up a finger to tell him
she would only be a moment.

Her face was so open. She smiled, she frowned, and
every thought was out there for all to see. And as he
watched her face became more familiar and comfortable
every second. It was not long before he felt as if he knew
every expression her lovely face could generate.

Finally, she came over and slumped into a chair beside
him and at once in such close proximity, away from the
beer and the sweaty men, a sudden sweet scent drifted his
way. It was heady and rich, like jasmine. It was her. And
it rocked him.

Trouble. The word rang unbidden in his head. Without
even trying, this one could prove to be a whole truckload
of trouble. He should go. Back to his corporate box. Back
to the office. Back to the other side of the world.

He should. But he couldn't. Not yet, anyway.

'You are a workhorse, Ms Denison,' he said, his tone
chatty.

'All for the good of the racecourse,' she said.

'And all for the good of Cloud Nine's coffers.'

'Not this one, I'm afraid. This one is my own little baby
and Cloud Nine have learnt to look the other way.'

'You are doing all this for nothing?'

'Don't get me wrong. I'm not footing the bill for all this grandeur. The costs for the day will come out of the takings, but I promise it will turn a very tidy profit.'

'Of which you will see not a cent?' Jacob could not believe he had heard right.

Holly laughed. 'You are such a doubting Thomas, Mr Lincoln. I promise I will not see even forty cents for a phone call.'

'Why?'

'These fundraisers make enough every year to keep the place running. If I took my usual percentage the day would be redundant.'

'But why here? Why this place? You said before you never bet. Do you just love the greyhounds that much?'

She pulled a face. 'Not at all. The whole half-starved puppies chasing a rabbit thing doesn't do it for me. It's just for the colonel, really.'

'How do you know him so well?'

She opened her mouth to answer but seemed to think better of it. She glanced around as though searching for a reason, or maybe a change of subject, and seemed to visibly relax when she saw the colonel coming her way.

'Holly, my sweet!' he said, his arms outstretched, ready to take her in.

She stood and gave the old man a big hug. Jacob felt an uncomfortable contraction in his chest at the sudden change in her. With him she was still the cool, confident, modern Melbourne woman, but in the company of the right person she blossomed into a completely different creature. Her smiles were softer, sweeter, with an abundant capacity for effortless delight.

'Charlie. Are you having a good time?'

'Always, my pet.'

'Are you ready for your speech? You are up in about ten minutes.'

'No problem. You are a sweet girl.' The colonel turned to Jacob. 'Our little mascot she was, always running around underfoot. Long hair flying behind her as she ran about the grandstands collecting old tickets, looking for the one that got away.'

A snippet of conversation from the grandstand snuck back into Jacob's consciousness. Not knowing how to fit the mismatched pieces into her story, he felt the fragment flutter away.

'And look at that little scar.' The colonel pointed at the bridge of Holly's nose and, though she swatted his hand away playfully, Jacob thought he saw a moment of panic in her action. 'Barely there now. All healed.'

Holly cut the colonel off, grabbing him around the middle and dragging him away, rolling her expressive blue eyes behind his back. 'Anyway, Charlie, it's all well and good taking us down amnesia lane, but it's time to get you to the stage. Excuse us, Jacob.'

And this time when she smiled it was just for him. And he knew, despite his very sensible inner protests, he was not going anywhere any time soon.

The colonel's speech went brilliantly. It was funny, sweet, and tender enough to have those listening make enough donations to run the old Hidden Valley Greyhound Course for another good year.

Jacob and Ben had waited for Holly. The other guys had gone back to the city to finish off their celebration, minus their guest of honour, and Holly offered to drop the two men home.

As the sun set over the all but empty racecourse they crossed the track in companionable silence. The ground had dried somewhat and they were all now in regular foot-wear. Though Holly, in her high heels, had a little trouble matching their long strides.

'Isn't this where you are supposed to lay down your coats for me?' she asked the men.

'I thought that was only for a queen,' Ben said from a few steps ahead of them.

'And we know you are only a princess,' Jacob whispered against her ear, sending thrilling hot shivers down the back of her neck. Holly poked out her tongue, though inside she was feeling far from flippant.

No matter how often she reminded herself of her perfectly good theory, she was beginning to sense there was more going on behind Jacob's taciturn gaze than she had at first thought. For instance, what sort of man would have the strength of personality to be able to persuade an alcoholic to drink lemonade in a public bar?

But maybe that was not the point. Maybe the theory just needed a little tweak. Maybe her archetypal Mr Standoffish *was* born with a conscience; just not with the commitment gene. He could be attractive as Adonis, and as intelligent as Plato, but would he be devoted as say, Ben?

That she very much doubted.

Jacob pressed a gentle hand to her back as they reached the gate to the car park. She leapt away from him as though his warm fingers were laced with fire. He did not seem to notice, he just kept herding her through the space and dropped his hand casually as they reached her car.

First Holly dropped Jacob back to the Lincoln Holdings offices where he was planning to put in a few more hours. He hopped out of the car, then peered through the driver window.

'Thanks for the lift.'

'No problem.' She had left the engine running at the ready for a quick getaway.

'And for the lovely afternoon. It was most…unexpected.'

She smiled, her lips tight, her hands clasping and unclasping the steering wheel. He was so close she could sense the remnants of his aftershave. Sweet and dry at the same time. Delicious.

He placed his hands on the bottom of the open window and leant in, his breath fanning her face as he spoke beyond her to Ben. 'See you tomorrow, Benny boy.'

Ben cocked his hand like a pistol. 'Shall do, boss.'

Jacob turned to Holly, his face still only inches from hers. It was all she could do not to close her eyes, drink in his delectable scent.

'I'll see you, Holly,' he said, and by his tone she believed it. He leant in and brushed a fleeting kiss upon her cheek. His lips were warm, soft, and gone all too soon. 'Promise me you will get Benny boy home to Beth in one piece.'

'I promise. Goodbye, Jacob.'

And as soon as his hands left the window she sped away. Allowing herself one brief glance in the rear-view mirror she saw Jacob standing in the road, his hands in his trouser pockets, watching her.

She kept her focus on the road ahead though her mind was spinning in another direction. 'Have you found *anyone* else to set me up with?'

Ben paused, as he seemed to absorb this question. 'I'm sure I could rustle up a couple of possibilities.'

'Then do it. As soon as possible.'

'If that's what you still want.'

'It is.' He was watching her but she ignored him. She had said all she wanted to say on the matter.

'Consider it done.'

She nodded, then drove Ben home to his waiting wife.

CHAPTER EIGHT

THANK GOD it's Friday, Holly thought as the drinks waiter handed over her champagne glass of lemon, lime, bitters, and a dash of honey. She savoured a long, thankful taste before looking over the room. All of the guests at the Arty Pants Modern Art Gallery Charity Evening were smiling, chatting, and paying a good deal of attention to the art. All was well.

Until one man in the corner smiled her way. A man in an expensive suit, blond hair thinning and styled to within an inch of its life, strong tan, perfect teeth. Holly's smile faded.

Oh, boy, not another one. Do they pop out of an assembly line just to attend parties and openings and corroborate my theory?

The man raised his glass in salute. Holly gave him a short polite nod and then moved away.

Luckily Lydia had just arrived, back from a week assisting at a Star Trek conference in Sydney.

'Hello, gorgeous!' Lydia called out as though she were on the other side of the room, not leaning into Holly's arms for a fond embrace. 'Loving it all, Holl. Great food, fabulous music and a feast for the eyes. Speaking of which, that blond dish in the corner is eyeing you up.'

Holly shot a quick glance at the man. He was still watching her over his tumbler.

'Sorry, Lydia. Not interested.'

Lydia raised a thin blonde eyebrow in disbelief. 'Why? Do you have something better lined up for dinner already?'

'Hardly. The truth is, while you were away Ben set me up on a spate of blind dates and the thought of telling my life story one more time makes me feel sick to the stomach.'

'So the husband hunt is off to a flying start, hey?'

Holly shrugged.

'Of course, while you were off having wildly romantic nights with dozens of men, I was fending off pointy eared, eight-foot geeks in rubber masks. Though there was this one Klingon...' She smiled slowly, before shaking her head clear. 'Anyway, please renew my hope in mankind. Tell me they were all delicious.'

Holly laughed. 'Tiresome, more like.'

'Hmm. Tiresome, were they?' Lydia waved a hand, indicating her question related entirely to bedroom pursuits.

Holly grabbed the offending hand. 'Lydia!'

'Come on, then. Gory details, please. I expect to be swooning at the end of this.'

'No promises, but here goes. Wednesday's guy took me to a restaurant where we had to sit on the floor, which was fine, until he removed his shoes. Foot odour competing with curry is not a scent I will soon forget.'

'So buy him cotton socks. Ooh, and you could wash his feet every night. Terribly sexy. Next!'

'Okay. Last night my blind date picked me up from work. Nice car. Nice conversation. Nice guy. Until he took me via home to meet his mother. And that was before dinner.'

'You are too picky. Mummy's boys can be wonderful. I'll bet he even cooks and cleans.'

'You think I'm too picky? Well, then, beat this, one gentleman offered to sire me a football team.'

Lydia's effusive laugh rang across the room so that several people turned their way. 'Now that one is a definite keeper. If you don't want him, give him my number.'

Holly felt an unwelcome prickling in her stomach at the thought of giving Lydia's phone number to that particular blind date.

'I guess this means fending off next-morning phone calls from panting men is back on my job description.'

Holly did not have the opportunity to refute Lydia's claim as her acquaintance's eyes were fixedly focussed on something, or someone, beyond her shoulder.

'Now that tasty morsel was worth coming along for.' The younger woman nodded coyly at the vision behind Holly.

'Who?' Holly spun around to catch a glimpse of the object of Lydia's divided attention. She could not hide her gasp at the sight of Jacob Lincoln ridding himself of his coat by the front door.

Lydia whirled straight back to Holly. 'You know him, I take it.'

'Barely.' Holly turned away from the door, her cheeks heating madly, her eyes scanning the room for safe ground.

'Holl, you have a shockingly ineffective poker-face, you know. And if you are thinking you can avoid introducing us now, you are sorely mistaken.'

Lydia grabbed Holly by the elbow and spun her around to face the door. Together they watched the man straighten his tie, smile at the hat-check girl as he took his ticket, and then look up, overtly searching the room.

It took only a moment for Jacob to catch sight of the two women near the bar. The younger woman with the mop of blonde curls and hot pink feather boa wrapped around her thin shoulders was practically beckoning him with her eyes, whereas the woman with the sleek chestnut hair and vibrant form-hugging dress in a mix of eye-popping blues and greens seemed to be finding her shoes extremely fascinating.

Jacob took a deep breath, straightened his tense shoulders, pocketed his coat-check ticket, and made a beeline towards them.

Jacob's usually confident gaze was flicking from side to side, his hands were clenching and unclenching in his trouser pockets and Holly knew he was, for once, unsure of himself. Amongst the bohemian crowd in which Holly felt totally at ease, Jacob was visibly unnerved, just as she had been amongst the beer, boxing and betting.

She smiled. Now they were even.

Holly guessed he probably felt more than a little over-dressed, but he was disarming in his black dinner suit, crisp white shirt and lavender tie. He oozed masculinity amongst the eclectic group of buyers, dealers, artists, and hangers-on, standing out like a prize bull in a field of mangy goats.

He nodded his hello.

Holly nodded back, though her brisk glance barely connected with his. She could feel Lydia grinning enormously beside her and soon received a distinct jab in the ribs.

'Jacob, this is my assistant, Lydia Lane. Lydia, this is Jacob Lincoln of Lincoln Holdings.'

Lydia offered her thin hand to Jacob, hot pink fingernails glinting in the created light. 'Enchanted, Jacob.'

'The pleasure's all mine, Lydia,' Jacob said, his tentative smile showcasing his dimples.

'I never knew the man behind the name would be so young, and so damnably attractive. Either way, you are a breath of fresh air blowing into this old crowd.'

Holly tried hard not to laugh aloud at Lydia's lavish efforts at sophistication.

Jacob leaned in closer to Lydia, his voice secretive. 'I've never actually been to one of these evenings before.'

'Really?' Lydia whispered back. 'Why are you here to-night, then?'

'I was invited by the kind people of Cloud Nine Event Management.'

Holly looked up, her eyes narrowed, and finally connected fully with his. 'No, you weren't.'

Lydia coughed back a scandalized laugh.

'I mean, I don't remember seeing your name on the guest list,' Holly said more tactfully.

Jacob reached into his jacket pocket and pulled out his invitation. Holly grabbed it and saw that it was addressed to the chairman of the Find Families Homes Foundation, the main beneficiary of the night's takings. Her eyes flew back to his.

'That's you?'

'That's me.'

'But they're wonderful.'

'Meaning I'm not?'

Drowning in Jacob's amused eyes, Holly gulped down a lump that had begun to hinder her breathing. She looked to her drink for inspiration and, finding only bubbles that matched the sensations in her stomach, she reached deeper for an explanation.

'No, I mean they are so kind, one of my…Cloud Nine's favourites. Their board always sends the most *wonderful* appreciative notes of thanks for our efforts but they have never sent a representative to the actual events.'

'Well, I'm here now, aren't I?' The tinge of a Louisiana accent leant his naturally deep voice a captivating drawl and it washed like an intimate caress over her bare shoulders.

'Looks like someone did not do her research,' Lydia said. 'Not my fault, of course. I've been out of town.'

Jacob grinned.

'I have a question for you, Jacob. Lincoln Holdings runs all events in-house, don't they?' Lydia asked. 'Why is that?'

Trust Lydia to get straight to the point. Holly pricked up her ears, very interested in the answer.

'I like to stay in control, so I keep my interests close. I find no point in outsourcing work when I can usually do it better.'

Holly openly scoffed.

'Though Holly and I will agree to disagree on that point.'

'If you are not simply an A-list party-goer, and have no use for her professional expertise, how do you know my gorgeous young friend here?' Lydia asked.

'We've only met briefly once or twice...' Holly mumbled.

'Mutual friends set us up on a blind date...' Jacob answered.

The two spoke over the top of each other, with Jacob's deep, clear voice coming out on top. Holly groaned, wishing she had not felt the need to entertain Lydia with her blind-date disaster stories earlier.

'Oh, you have to be kidding!' Lydia jumped up and down on the spot, clapping her hands in glee, her ringlets bobbing up and down, all efforts at sophistication blown. And Holly knew Lydia would sooner not breathe than not comment.

'Were you the guy with the live-in mother or the one who is planning on keeping Holly with child for the next decade? If he's the one with the foot odour, Holl, I'd wash this man's feet morning, noon and night.'

The one with the live-in mother? The one with foot odour? Had Holly been on further blind dates since meeting him? Ben had not mentioned a word of it. True, he had not asked Ben, just assuming the misguided idea would have lost its momentum by now.

But there had been others. And though that meant she was still forging ahead on her mad husband hunt, which he wanted no part of, he found he did not like the thought of her seeing other men one little bit.

'Come on,' Lydia repeated, 'which one were you?'

Holly watched Jacob under lowered eyelashes. Since Lydia's outburst, a small muscle in his cheek had been clenching and unclenching and his bright eyes were clouded by shadow. He turned an enigmatic smile her way, his stare so focussed it knocked the breath from her lungs.

'Well,' he said, his deadpan gaze never leaving her face, 'I hope I'm the one who spoilt her for all others.'

Holly's mouth flew open wide, ready to deny the ludicrous statement outright, knowing Lydia would otherwise lap it up.

And then it dawned on her. That was exactly what he had done. On her other dates she had been distracted. When they had picked her up, her mind had wandered to the night in the foggy street. When they had sat down to dinner she'd remembered Jacob in his impeccable suit, wearing those ridiculous yellow galoshes at the greyhound track. When they'd spoken they'd been drowned out by memories of Jacob's smooth, sonorous voice, rich with charm and that barely there accent.

She had not been looking for problems on her dates, but

looking for ways in which those men could measure up to this one. Having experienced his intelligence, wicked sense of humour, and looks so fine they made her knees weak every time she caught him even glancing her way, she was finding it hard to accept less in the other men she met.

But he so clearly did not match her criteria. Too detached, too independent, too…too much. Not like Ben in the least. And Ben was her yardstick when it came to husband material.

'How was the date, really?' Lydia said, breaking the silence.

'It was entirely dreadful…' Holly said.

'It was quite promising…' Jacob said.

And again, his answer came through loud and clear.

'Promisingly dreadful or dreadfully promising?' Lydia asked.

Before either could answer, Lydia's attention was drawn elsewhere. 'There's the superb St John. I have to congratulate him on his ace lithographs. I'll leave you two sweet young things to yourselves, then, shall I?'

Lydia left in a cloud of youthful perfume and floating pink feathers, and once more Holly was alone with Jacob. She knew she should bid him good evening and walk away. The less time spent in his complicated company, the better.

She searched for a way out, someone requiring her professional attention. But she only found the simpering blond gentleman eyeing her like a hawk. She glanced back at Jacob and in a heartbeat knew the blond would be the safer option.

But it was too late. She was drawn into Jacob's resolute hazel gaze and found herself rooted to the spot. She could not blame her bubbling drink for the hot flush creeping across her bare neck, as she had been drinking nothing bar lemon, lime and bitters with a dash of honey all night.

Jacob watched in fascination as the faint blush swept across Holly's delicate shoulders. He felt an unrelenting urge to stroke a cool hand along her neck to feel its warmth. Her face hid nothing of the tumult raging inside her and he was amazed. Amazed at her strong physical reaction to him, though not amazed at how much he enjoyed it.

'Why did you really come tonight?' Holly asked, her eyes hiding none of her uncertainty.

Jacob plunged his hands deep into his pockets, knowing from her tone they were safer there than coming anywhere near this volatile vixen.

'I had an opening in my calendar and the invitation offered free canapés.' Jacob knew his flippant responses would wear thin, but he had no intention of telling her he had spent so much time thinking about her he was getting little work done.

The truth was he had decided the only fix was to see her again. The fantasy girl he had progressively built in his head over the last couple of days could only be toppled once tempered by the real thing. The bundle of nerves before him.

The husband hunter—who it turned out was infinitely more tempting up close and personal than even her fantasy version.

'Where can a man get a drink around here?' He searched the room, saw the small bar, and taking Holly by the elbow, led her to the counter. 'Another for the lady and the same for me, please.'

'It's not champagne,' Holly said.

'That's okay by me. You don't drink?'

'Not when I'm working, no.'

He had forgotten for a moment she was working. Foolishly, he had been lulled into feeling as if they were just out for a drink. He and Holly, together.

Mistake.

Holly played with one of her dangly turquoise earrings as she turned to chat to the head beverage waiter, making sure the guests had so far been happy on the drinks front.

Jacob used the quiet moment to focus, to get back to the real reason he had come. The fact that she was on the lookout for a husband was not proving to be a big enough barrier to his temptation any more. So he took a good look at her, with every intention of finding as many faults as it would take to render her unappealing.

Her customary fringe was slicked from a dramatic side parting across her forehead, and hair was drawn into a low heavy bun at her nape, leaving her creamy shoulders bare. He wished she would wear her hair down for once. There, that was a fault. Wasn't it?

With a critical eye his gaze moved lower, meandering down the delectable curves enhanced by her stunning, sleek, psychedelic dress. The lustrous fabric fell to the top of her feet, thus hiding her lovely legs. She covered them too often. He knew he was stretching to find a fault with that, but a fault it had to be.

And then, as though she sensed the direction of his gaze, Holly's hand left her earring and ran down her leg to her foot, unconsciously rubbing the insole. Watching, enthralled, Jacob caught a glimpse of a simple gold toe ring on one sandalled foot and it surprised him. A touch of the gypsy amidst her cool glamour. He let out a deep breath, the simple frivolity of that one piece of jewellery promising so much more. So much hidden. So much waiting to be discovered.

* * *

Through her entire conversation Holly had been sure Jacob's eyes had not left her and as such she had barely been able to concentrate on the poor waiter, having to ask him to repeat himself on more than one occasion.

But when she looked up Jacob's wide eyes were on the waiter, who was dipping a teaspoon in and out of their drinks.

'Is that honey?' he asked.

Holly merely raised her eyebrows as if to say, *You asked for it.* She took her drink and sipped at it happily.

Jacob took his, sniffed at it, stared at it, and shook the glass. And even put his ear close to listen to it.

'Why don't you just try drinking it?' Holly said, her voice full of laughter.

'And why don't you sit down for a second?'

'Fair enough.' Holly slid onto the bar stool next to his. She groaned in gratification as she eased the weight off her sore feet. 'So, why did you come back from overseas?'

'The time was right.'

She nodded, though she wanted more information. More background. Just more.

'And with your sister's impending marriage, I bet she's happy.'

'She is.' For a brief second he let down his guard and Holly saw the genuine affection he held for his sister. His face glowed with it. And it was lethally charming.

Now that was a definite chink in her theory. This guy was meant to have no attachments. He could be devoted to his business. Or even passionate about his car. But he was not meant to radiate such tenderness when talking of another person.

Hang on. The theory could still hold true; she would just have to make another slight modification. Blood relatives were an exception to the 'no attachments' rule. That seemed only fair.

'And the company?' she continued. 'Were your employees pleased to see you? Though it does mean they will have to start actually working, stop the three-hour lunches, and fire the in-house masseuse that Ben always raves about.'

'Are you kidding? That's the main reason I'm back.' He touched his hand to the back of his neck. 'I've had this dull ache in my third vertebra...'

'Sure you have.'

Feeling cosy and safe in the conversation, she could not stop herself from asking the question that had been foremost in her mind for the last few days.

'So are you here to stay?'

The sparkle left Jacob's eyes as he considered her for a long, agonising moment. Her heart seemed to stop beating as she awaited the answer.

'For now.'

She nodded, though her inappropriate angst had not been assuaged one little bit.

As though sensing the sudden weight of the subject at hand, Jacob turned the conversation to more ordinary issues. They talked about the gallery, and surprisingly Jacob knew a lot about the resident artist. He even had one of 'the superb St John's ace lithographs' in his apartment.

Her feet lightly aching, Holly once more ran a massaging palm over the arch of her foot.

'Long day?' Jacob asked.

'Long week.'

'Too many nights out, I think.'

She stopped rubbing and sat up, slowly, not looking his way. 'And I'd have to agree with you.'

'Maybe you should cut back?'

'Maybe I should.'

Holly's pulse was racing. The swirl of meaning behind their innocuous conversation reverberated in the air around them. Was he asking her not to see other men? Was she agreeing? Was she mad?

'What if...?' Jacob said, his voice trailing off.

What if, what? Holly thought, her nerves screaming in anticipation. She felt like a bell still resonating long after it had been struck.

'Dinner. Tomorrow night. Just you and me.' Jacob turned on his seat, his left hand coming down to rest upon hers. 'No strings. Just dinner.'

His little finger was stroking, playing, tantalising, sending hot, jolting shivers from her sensitive fingertips up her bare arms, melting the length of her suddenly rigid body. And then he smiled. *Strength, Holly. A smile is teeth and lips and muscles. Nothing more.*

'I won't demand any feet-washing at the end of the night. Unless of course you feel the urge...'

She pulled her hand away. She wanted strings. That was the whole point. Holly stood up behind the bar stool, putting herself a safe distance from his potent magnetism.

'It's never just dinner, Jacob. And neither should it be.'

'But—'

'But, you know my long-term plans. I want a husband. And you can't even tell me if you're still going to be in the country in a week, so I'm guessing marriage is not an option in your foreseeable future.'

All colour drained from Jacob's face and there was her answer. *So he loves his sister, so he supports charities, so he has a smile that liquefies all common sense. He is and always will be the indisputable anti-husband. There never was a safer bet.*

'I didn't think so. So there's really no point in having dinner, is there?'

For the sake of her own disobedient feelings she simply had to hit the point home as far as she could. So she lied. 'Besides which, you're simply not my type.'

Jacob blinked, his luscious eyelashes sweeping across his beautiful chiselled cheeks. 'And those other poor saps during the week. Did they have the same advance warning I did?'

Holly shrank back from the bitterness in Jacob's tone and she knew she was doing the right thing, cutting off all further contact before it was too late. Before he made such a deep impression on her she could not simply theorise it away.

'Goodbye, Jacob.'

Holly walked away, feeling Jacob's slighted stare burning into her as she crossed the room. She latched onto the owner of the gallery and he kept her sequestered in his bawdy, noisy group until long after Jacob had grabbed his coat and left.

CHAPTER NINE

MONDAY morning Holly's intercom buzzed.

'Call on line three, Ms Denison.' The receptionist's fuzzy voice came through the speakerphone on her desk.

Holly looked apologetically at Lydia, who was standing on a chair in the middle of her office, her outstretched arms draped in several large swatches of fabric. 'Do you mind hanging in there for a minute? I'll be quick.'

Lydia strained dramatically under the weight. 'Get it, Holly, I'm just *fine* up here.'

Holly grabbed the phone and swung back in her springy leather chair. 'Holly Denison.'

'Holly. It's Jacob.'

Holly shot forward on her chair, her feet now both firmly planted on the ground. He needn't have introduced himself. That rich, masculine voice with its gentle American twang set her nerves on edge from its very first syllable.

Lydia raised her eyebrows and mouthed, 'Who is it?'

Holly shook her head, before pressing the phone firmly to her ear. After Friday night Holly had spent a restless weekend convincing herself turning him down was for the best.

But three little words were enough to have her doubting herself again. And if he was calling to ask her to dinner again, she did not know if she would have the strength to refuse.

'Yes, Jacob?'

'I have a party to organise and I want to employ your professional services for the event.'

She scribbled, *Lincoln Holdings—party* onto her note-pad.

Lydia could see the notebook clearly from her elevated position and her jaw dropped. Holly waved a frantic hand at her mouthing for her to dump the fabric swatches over the back of the chair and disappear.

Lydia mouthed, 'Good luck,' before she tiptoed out.

So he had not called to renew his dinner offer. Holly was glad he was not there in person to see her blush. He had obviously taken her at her word on that count. But that was what she wanted. Wasn't it?

Then it hit her what he *had* requested. Jacob Lincoln was offering Cloud Nine a gig. But she knew his idea of a party was very different from her own. She shuddered at the thought of having to search the local bars and pubs for a venue and putting up posters advertising a wet T-shirt contest with a free keg of beer being the first prize.

'I am flattered that you thought of Cloud Nine for the event, Jacob, but I'm not sure we provide the sort of parties that would suit your tastes.'

Jacob surprised Holly by laughing loudly on the other end of the line. 'Relax, Holly. I'm not after nude mud wrestlers. Besides, this is not for the company. It's a private affair. My sister Ana wants an engagement party. Something much more along the lines of what you created for the big marquee would be appropriate.'

This sounded much more up her professional alley but Holly knew that the theme of the party was not what was really worrying her.

'Well, I am extremely busy at the moment but I could pass you on to another of our wonderful event managers who specializes in exactly these sort of—'

'Look, Holly—' his voice seemed to lose all patience '—this is just the beginning of what I am proposing here. If I like what you do with this gig, I will be offering you the entire Lincoln Holdings event management account.'

Holly blinked. Slowly. If she had had the strength, she would have pinched herself.

'The entire Lincoln Holdings account?' she repeated.

'Yes. We have been able to handle the workload internally until now but the company is leaping ahead internationally and the job is getting too big.'

Holly desperately tried to rein in her imagination, which was running riot with wild ideas.

'What's the catch?' she asked, hoping there was a great big one so she would have a sane reason to refuse.

'The catch is I don't want anyone else in charge of my account. I want you.'

Be careful what you wish for, Holly, for you just might get it. Those words echoed through her head as she sat in stunned silence.

He was offering her an account that her firm, amongst dozens of others, had been wooing without success for years. There was no way she could seriously convince herself or anyone else that she should turn this opportunity down. She had to do this party and it had to be perfect.

She sighed aloud. 'All right. I'll do it.'

'Don't sound so eager, please.' He laughed.

'I am, don't get me wrong. This is a huge opportunity. Though I can't help but wonder why.'

'Why not?' Jacob asked.

'Well, you've seen my work. And we both know I don't have the same tastes as you.' *And we all but had a fight the other night. And I had thought I might not ever hear that divine voice of yours again.*

Jacob laughed again and Holly grimaced, aware that she was fast finding the sound addictive.

'You really know how to sell yourself, don't you? I'm beginning to change my mind about the whole deal.'

Holly could not help but laugh as well. 'Look, I will happily take on your sister's engagement party and don't get me wrong, I will knock your socks off, it will be that fabulous. But I have a counter proposal.'

'Okay, let's hear it.'

She took a deep breath and went for it. 'I will deal with your sister alone for this party and when you give me the Lincoln Holdings account, which I am sure you will, I will deal with your promotions division, and not with you.'

'Well, now, that was more like it,' Jacob said, 'I was not sure that you had that self-protective spirit in you.'

His voice had reached her a little softer and definitely sexier, which was not what Holly had been hoping to bring out in him. She had merely been establishing professional boundaries. Not something she had previously thought sexy, but with Jacob involved…

'Thank you, I think,' she said, her own voice huskily mirroring his own. She cleared her throat. 'If you could pass on your sister's number we can get started right away.'

Jacob gave her Ana's contact details. 'And whatever Ana wants, Ana gets. The result of my being away so long. I am trying to buy back her affection.'

Holly knew from the warmth of his voice that this statement could not be farther from the truth. And again she wondered what sort of woman could secure such staunch and palpable affection from this man.

'So long as I don't have to help Ana choose between bronze and pewter candleholders. I've been there and done that and it wasn't pretty.'

'Pewter,' Holly answered without pause as she continued scribbling burgeoning ideas onto her notepad.

'See, that's just what she eventually chose. I think you two were made for each other.'

'*I think* if you promised to stay for ever she would prefer that to a party any day.'

Where on earth had *that* come from? Holly clamped a hand to her mouth to stop any further recriminating rubbish from slipping out.

'Would *she* now?' His voice whispered down the phone line silky smooth. The insinuation in his question clear.

Holly rubbed her suddenly throbbing temples. 'Ask her, Jacob,' she said, pretending she had no idea what he had implied, 'and see what she says.'

'I am sure you are right,' he said, his voice mercifully back to normal. 'I guess I'll wait to hear from Ana, then, to see how it's all going.'

'I would appreciate that. And Jacob?'

'Yes, Holly.'

'Thank you.'

'Don't thank me yet,' he warned her before hanging up the phone.

Holly put the phone down more slowly. Lydia was peering through the glass door with a big expectant grin on her face. Holly waved her into the room.

'So?' Lydia asked, her eyes bright with excitement.

'It may soon be safe to dummy up a press release saying we've landed the Lincoln Holdings account.'

'Yippee!' Lydia spun around in glee before slumping down on the chair she had been standing on earlier, the important swathes of fabric temporarily forgotten.

'You had no plans day or night for the next few weeks, did you?' Holly asked.

Lydia waved a 'no worries' hand. 'The Klingon can wait.'

Holly thought it better not to ask. 'The sooner we ready our other projects, the sooner we can reel in Jacob Lincoln.'

'You mean Lincoln Holdings, don't you?'

'Of course I do.' Holly swiftly changed the subject. 'Now, up you get, back on the chair so we can sort out these fabrics before lunch.'

Lydia grumbled as she stood back up on the chair and stretched out her aching arms, 'Sometimes I feel highly unappreciated.'

'I can't believe you just did that,' Ben said from Jacob's office doorway.

Jacob knew from Ben's smug expression he had been listening for long enough. 'Believe it, Benny boy. It's become too big for me and I've been contemplating outsourcing for some time.' *For three whole days, in fact.*

'This is the first I had heard of it.'

'This is the first you needed to hear of it. That's why the company is my namesake and not yours.'

Ben sauntered into the room, and then lay back on a lounge chair against the far wall. He nonchalantly flipped through a magazine on Jacob's coffee-table. 'She didn't go on any dates this weekend, you know. I had a couple of men lined up, including the new Accounts guy, Matt Riley, the one who tried chatting her up at the greyhound track. But she baulked.'

There is no reason why that should concern me, Jacob thought, then realised he had stopped breathing.

'And young Matt's quite the looker, I am told by the girls in Accounts,' Ben continued. '*Babeliscious* I think was the most common turn of phrase. Modelled his way through college, you know? But…still she said no.'

Ben's eyes left the magazine and zeroed in on Jacob, who hoped his face showed none of the curiosity he felt.

'You wouldn't happen to know why she has suddenly backed off, would you?' Ben asked.

Jacob merely shook his head, uncertain what state his voice would be in considering his suddenly dry throat. Maybe she had given up the hunt and had decided to become a normal single woman, capable of organising her own social life. Now that would be an interesting turn of events.

Then Ben said, 'Maybe she just needed to recharge her batteries. Ready herself for next week's multitude of contenders.'

'Maybe,' Jacob conceded, thumping briskly back to earth.

'Well, it's been easier than I thought it would be. She really made an impression on the bunch at your welcome home thing at the track. Once word got around *she* was open to being set up, I've hardly had to do a thing.'

'Lucky you.'

'Yep. I've met all sorts of great guys this last week. I had to cancel one guy's date but *we* got on so well I booked him in for a conciliatory lunchtime squash game.'

Jacob was determined not to give Ben the satisfaction of knowing that his comments were surprisingly hitting the mark. He was actually feeling pangs of something akin to jealousy.

'Was there something else I could help you with?'

Ben looked to the ceiling for inspiration. 'Nope.'

'I can find work for you if you're bored. I don't think my blinds have been cleaned in the years I've been gone.'

Ben looked at his watch. 'Sorry, Link. I'll be late for squash with my new friend.'

He stood and ambled back to the door before looking back with an easy grin. 'Just think, if Holly had not been run down by that oaf in the street the other week and been so turned off by him as to go on this husband hunt of hers, I would be eating lunch alone in my office right now. You've got to love the girl!'

'Who's an oaf?' Jacob called out but Ben had already gone.

So, Holly had been turned off by the 'oaf' in the street, had she? Jacob fumed. He grabbed a stick of gum and chewed it furiously as he swung sharply back and forth in his office chair.

No wonder she had begged him not to tell Beth they had met before. Turned off! She had been practically undressing him with her eyes that first morning, he was certain of it. The little fraud. She deserved to be found out for twisting that incident to suit her.

Unless she really had found him repellent from their first meeting. Every time he had seen her since she had been edgy and had made it clear she would rather be anywhere than in his presence. And she had flung the 'not her type' line in his face with convincing vigour.

All the better for him if that was the end of it. No use wasting time struggling to bat down his growing attraction to the woman if he held no appeal for her in the first place.

And then he stopped, mid swing, his feet planted firmly on the carpeted floor, and his hands grabbed his desk as he realised what Ben had unwittingly revealed. The one detail that made all of the above possibilities irrelevant.

He was the reason behind Holly's whole husband hunt.

*   *   *

'That's great Holly! What a coup,' Beth said over the phone later that night. 'And you'll love Ana.'

'Please tell me you can come.'

'Of course. Unless the baby makes other plans we'll be there with bells on.'

'Bells will not be necessary. Evening wear will be fine.'

Holly sat on her bed in her shortie pyjamas and thick socks, assuming the lotus position. She held the cordless phone to her ear, and rocked her neck back and forth easing out the niggling Monday-itis tensions.

'Ben tells me you cancelled on two of your hopefuls on the weekend.'

'Hmm. I needed a break.'

'Really? No other reason? No one take your fancy yet from the hundreds Ben has supplied?'

Holly heard the doubt in Beth's voice loud and clear. 'No one.'

'Not even Jacob?'

'Beth—'

'Come on, Holly. If it weren't for Ben I would grab the man with both hands and not let him go. He's the catch to end all catches.'

'You would not. He's so not your type.'

'Then whose is he?'

Holly let that one slide. 'And besides I feel like a movie star doing the talk show circuit. I need to come up with some new material before even I am bored with my funny stories.' After one final stretch Holly flopped backwards, her arms and legs spread diagonally across the bed.

'As long as this plan of yours has not fizzled out,' Beth said.

'I promise there has been no fizzling.'

'Good, because I had already decided that my matron of honour dress was going to be bright red, backless and very sparkly. Besides I did up a current star chart and you are primed for a liaison in July. In fact you are so primed you are about to burst. Maybe tarots would help—'

'No! I draw the line at tarot cards.'

Beth sighed. 'Fine. What are you doing tonight? Watching TV?'

Alone? Holly felt the inference come through loud and clear. She glanced at the silent TV at the end of her bed. 'If it weren't for your Ben we would still be a pair of old spinsters who loved to do nothing more at night than watch *Pride and Prejudice* and eat home-made caramel popcorn.'

'That was fun, though, wasn't it?'

'The most fun ever. But then Ben found you, and loved you and showed both of us how much better our nights could be.'

Holly sighed. She rolled over and scrunched herself into a warm little ball, with the phone cradled under her head. 'I've seen *Pride and Prejudice* enough times for one woman. You don't know how lucky you are, Beth. To have someone so decent and strong and dependable.'

Beth laughed. 'You make Ben sound like a St Bernard!'

Better a St Bernard than a Rottweiler, she thought as images of Jacob Lincoln with his dark hair, clear sharp eyes and his overwhelming personality bombarded her subconscious.

'Someone like Ben would drive you around the bend,' Beth said.

'Hardly—'

'For example, he keeps his socks, underpants and hankies in the same dresser drawer. You have a separate drawer for each and organise them by colour and fabric with seasonal adjustments.'

'How will I ever be able to look at Ben again without thinking about his underwear?'

'Seriously, though, one day you will meet the man for you. A man who puts honey in everything he cooks. A man who will be happy to let you name your first-born son Maximus as you have always wanted, God help the poor child.'

'I don't see what is so wrong with the name Maximus. It's a powerful and masculine name—'

'Will you stop kidding around and listen to me?'

Duly chastised, Holly shut up and paid attention.

'What I am saying is the perfect man for you is out there. But believe me he will be nothing like Ben. That's nothing against my husband. You drive him around the bend just the same.'

'Thanks.'

And Holly knew then that, though her friends would always be there with a shoulder to lean on, it would in all likelihood fall to her to find someone to love.

CHAPTER TEN

AT LUNCHTIME on Tuesday Holly escorted Lydia to the Lunar restaurant to meet Anabella for their first chat about her upcoming engagement party. Holly had spoken to Ana on the phone that morning and had found her bright and excited and was very much looking forward to meeting her.

Holly ordered her usual lemon, lime, and bitters with a touch of honey and Lydia ordered a pink lemonade spider with double whipped cream and chocolate topping.

Soon after Jacob Lincoln slid his impressive suit-clad frame onto the leather bench opposite her.

'Jacob! What on earth are you doing here?'

Why? Why are you here? Holly screamed inside her head. *Wasn't I perfectly clear? Did you not promise to leave the party to me? Without interference? Without walking in here unheralded, smiling at me like that, like a naughty little boy who knows his mother would never yell at him as long as he flashed those adorable dimples.*

Knowing she had been staring far too long, Holly glanced furtively at Lydia, and was glad to see she was being blithely ignored. In fact, as Lydia lowered her lipstick to her attaché case and smoothed her newly glossed lips together her wide eyes never left Jacob for a moment.

'I beg you not to throw that drink in my face, Holly,' Jacob said. He sent her an enigmatic smile, as though he knew something she didn't. 'New suit. And Anabella sends her apologies but she suddenly had to go out of town...for a week.'

Holly had to pull herself together. Lydia was now watching the two of them very carefully. 'I spoke to her only this morning and she didn't say a thing.'

Jacob shrugged. 'As I said, it was sudden.'

'And her fiancé? He was unable to come in her place?'

'Well, he actually had to suddenly go out of town as well. With Anabella. Skiing in New Zealand.'

'I see,' she said, desperately seeking a way to take control of the situation. 'So why didn't she just cancel our meeting until she comes back?'

'She wants the party booked for Saturday week but won't be back in Melbourne until midday on the day before. She gave me these notes and said to follow them as a guide, but she would be happy with whatever you come up with.'

He reached over the table with a few loose sheets of pink writing paper covered with loopy handwriting. Lydia's hand slid across the table and snapped them up.

'I have a week and a half to organise a party for...how many people?' Holly asked.

Lydia, who was poring over the pink pages, said, 'Three hundred.'

'Three hundred people?'

'Of course it's people, though it doesn't specifically say people in the notes—'

'Lydia!'

'We can do it easily, Holly,' Lydia said. 'Remember the Newman do? We did that in just over a week and it was fab.'

Holly glared at Lydia, who just shrugged.

'What did I say? It's true.'

Holly sensed Jacob watching them, his head swaying back and forth as though watching a tennis match.

'Look, if you think you need help or if I should get someone else to do it—' he said.

Holly placed her hands steadily on the table in front of her. 'No, we will be fine.'

The waiter arrived and asked if they were ready to order lunch. Jacob raised his eyebrows at Holly and his look said it all. He had laid his cards on the table; he had changed the rules and made no promises he would not do so again. So much for professional boundaries.

But now it was her move. Order the meal or don't order the meal. Take the deal or don't take the deal. It was decision time and it was up to her.

So Holly ordered.

Soup of the day with a side salad. It would be served quickly and could be eaten quickly. Besides, the way her stomach was reacting she probably would not keep anything heavier down.

Jacob ordered appetisers and eye fillet steak. Well done. 'Cook it till it's unrecognisable,' he said, 'then flip it and cook it some more.'

'You should eat it rare. It's much better for you.' Holly nodded frantically at the waiter, willing him to change the order. Jacob shot her that peculiar enigmatic smile again and she shut up.

Lydia took a long, luxurious sip of her drink, the liquid gurgling loudly as it reached the bottom of the glass, then ordered a slice of apple pie with ice cream. 'The sugar stimulates me,' she explained.

Jacob laughed aloud and the young male waiter had to stifle a cough as he left.

'So how have you been, Lydia?' Jacob asked.

'Fabulous, Jacob. And you?'

'Fabulous.' His urbane voice gave the casual word a

whole different feel. Long, drawn out, smooth. Holly took a large gulp of her drink.

'If you two are finished,' Holly said, 'let's talk about the party.' She stopped as Jacob held up his hands, his face contorted with mock apprehension.

'You promised me I wouldn't have to choose between pewter and bronze.'

'But—'

'No buts. Follow the notes if you must, but as I said on the phone you guys have carte blanche.'

It sounded perfect in theory, but Holly knew there was no way of pleasing a client without substantial input. One person's pewter was another person's bronze.

Obviously sensing the same looming disaster, Lydia whipped out the contract and gave it to Jacob. 'If you could just look this over, fill in your details and the party date, sign away and we have a deal.'

Jacob did as he was told, then Holly signed alongside his name. Lydia clapped her hands together excitedly as she took the signed contract and placed it carefully in her pink attaché case.

'Carte blanche,' Lydia cooed. 'My two favourite words in the whole English language.'

Jacob laughed aloud again. And Holly felt her skin resonating in response to the infectious sound.

'So, Jacob,' Lydia said, 'since we can't talk shop, tell me why you had to stop Holly from throwing her drink over you?'

His eyes crinkled. 'Well, I just knew that she was expecting my sister and didn't want her to freak out.'

'Holly, freak out?' Lydia scoffed. 'She's the coolest cucumber you could ever hope to meet.'

'Do tell.'

'Sure. I mean, take yesterday lunchtime; these expatriate

English people who were having a British-Australian dinner. We'd spent three full days with the client finalising
the seating arrangements. We had even printed up these
lovely table number cards. Weren't they lovely, Holly?'

'They were lovely, Lydia,' Holly agreed, flicking a
quick apologetic smile to Jacob, who winked briefly before
turning his rapt attention back to Lydia. Holly's skin tingled as though that wink had crossed the table and brushed
along her cheek. She crept a stealthy hand from her lap to
her face and rubbed at the wayward spot.

'Anyway,' Lydia continued, 'at the last minute the client
realised that Joe was at table number three and Eunice was
at table number four. They were both in the front row,
both within spitting distance of the speaker, but Joe was
sitting at a higher table number than Eunice. And this was
cataclysmic. The client was ready to cancel the whole
thing. In stepped Miss Cool Bananas here and said, Let's
just rename the tables; not numbers, not letters, but names
of small English towns. The client hyperventilated her
agreement. There went our Holly into her ''magic'' briefcase and found enough fancy paper and a black magic
marker to rename every table. And within minutes of
everyone's arrival the whole room was in tears as they
blabbed about the small English towns they all knew and
loved and missed. Even Joe and Eunice were hugging each
other and bawling their eyes out.'

Lydia took a deep breath and slumped back in her chair.
'Jacob, can you look around the corner and see if my apple
pie is coming? I'm starved!'

It took a moment for Jacob to latch onto Lydia's sudden
change of topic. He peeked. 'Not just yet.'

'Good. Holly, could you shove over for a sec? I have
to take a pee before my pie comes.'

Holly obligingly moved out of her seat so Lydia could

shuffle past. 'Thanks, gorgeous.' She flounced past Holly and skipped towards the ladies' room.

Holly slid back down into her seat, slowly and deliberately, already marking the seconds until Lydia's return.

'Isn't she exhausting?' Jacob said.

Talk about Lydia. Excellent. Safe ground.

'She's enthusiastic and imaginative and the clients love her. I'll probably end up working for her one day.'

After a moment's pause, during which time his mind seemed to be ticking over, Jacob asked, 'She called you "gorgeous". Ben and Beth both refer to you in that way as well. Do you just get that particular compliment a lot?'

'Hardly.'

Hardly a professional topic of conversation. Explain then change the subject.

'My dad called me that since I was little. And then one day when I first met Ben he called out "Hey, gorgeous" to Beth and I answered without even thinking. And he and Beth have called me that ever since. The guys at work heard Ben call me that at the Christmas party a couple of years ago and never let it go. I barely notice it any more.'

Jacob smiled. 'It suits you.'

'Please,' she scoffed, looking over her shoulder to check if Lydia was on her way back.

After another pregnant pause, Jacob thankfully changed the subject. 'Did you really do all those things she said? Yesterday lunchtime?'

'In a manner of speaking. Though she makes it seem much more exhilarating than it really was. It was a fairly simple fix and we've had worse problems closer to the final hour.'

'There you go, selling yourself short again.'

'Fine.' She laughed. 'I was brilliant. I saved the day.'

'That's better.'

'But it's my job to fix those things, to smooth the way and make the events seem effortless whilst the client sits back and takes the honour.'

Watch and learn, buddy. This party of Ana's will blow your mind.

Jacob sat back and crossed his arms, mirroring her stance. 'Do you see yourself branching out with your own firm?'

'I love what I do and if I was the owner I wouldn't be able to do it. I'd have to concentrate on finances and payroll and other such icky things. I'm happy to play with other people's money.'

'And this way you could more easily take time off if you needed it.'

'I guess.' She wondered why he would focus on that aspect. 'But it would be decidedly more difficult to make the house payments if I was skipping off on cruises year round.'

'You own a house?' His eyes softened as he asked.

'It will be a few years yet before I can claim that distinction from the bank.'

'I see. But, if your circumstances changed, you *could* stop working altogether,' Jacob added, his hazel eyes now boring into hers.

'I guess I could.'

If I pick the right lottery numbers, or find a suitcase of money buried in my backyard.

And then it dawned on her. He was thinking that what she wanted most in a job was the flexibility to marry and have children as soon as possible.

How wrong he was! Or was he?

If she followed her plan through to its logical conclusion, wouldn't that mean a wedding, a honeymoon, and some day children? Holly felt a comforting blush creep over her as these ideas filtered through and meshed with her original plan just to find someone nice and compatible to spend her time with. She loved her job but the thought of a full life with a real family was intoxicating.

But hang on. This was not Beth having an innocent chat, and not a prospective husband seeing where her priorities lay. This was the man who, *if she played her cards right*, would be going a long way to funding her pay cheques.

But would he seriously reconsider handing over the Lincoln Holdings account to her if she was planning to start a family? If so, he was completely outside his rights.

But, closer to home, would she seriously consider starting a family if it meant losing the Lincoln Holdings account, which epitomised all she had ever wanted from her career, something she had been striving for long before the notion of a husband hunt had presented itself.

But before she could open her mouth to contradict him, or berate him, or promise to give up the hunt as long as he gave her the contract, the waiter arrived with their lunch, quickly followed by Lydia.

'Did you miss me?' Lydia asked as she climbed over Holly's lap and plopped into her own seat.

'More than life itself,' Jacob promised, shooting one final unreadable glance at Holly before tucking into his appetizer.

Her mind reeling, Holly could do little more than pick up her spoon and eat her soup.

Jacob stood outside Lunar and watched as Holly's chauffeured car drove away, the icy wind whipping through his lightweight suit barely registered.

'Holly. Holly. Holly,' he whispered aloud, 'what is spinning though that labyrinthine mind of yours?' Holly's uneasy expression as she'd slipped into the back of the car was branded on his mind.

He reached into his inner jacket pocket and grabbed a stick of gum. He threw it into his mouth and chewed furiously and began to walk the five blocks back to the office.

The day had not gone exactly as he had hoped.

When he'd known he would be taking the lunch in Ana's place, he had imagined Holly would be glad to see him, keen to thank him in person for the incredible opportunity he had given her. After an hour spent flirting over lunch, he would then help her into a cab, her hand resting for a few extra moments in his, tears in her eyes, thanking her lucky stars she had met him and for him having bestowed such an opportunity on her.

Admittedly, that had been a little optimistic. But from the panic in her expression he had even worried that she was planning on reneging on the whole deal. That was the last thing he wanted. He had become used to the idea of her running a part of his show.

So what was wrong with her? Why couldn't she be thrilled with what he was offering her? For the first time in ten years, he was contemplating handing over the public face of his company. Didn't she understand that? Understand the incredible chance he had taken?

For her?

As he'd watched her reactions with a studied eye at lunch she had fidgeted, blushed, and avoided direct eye contact. He knew he definitely did not repulse her as she had apparently claimed to Ben. Nevertheless, whatever she had felt that morning on the street had caused a strong reaction in her, and she'd created her husband hunt as a wall, an excuse not to face those feelings.

Since he'd unwittingly slung her into her current predicament, maybe he was the only one who could release her. He was simply unable to give her what she wanted most. But he could supply the next best thing—the job she had always dreamed of.

A car beeped its horn as Jacob stepped out onto the road. The street sign read 'Don't Walk'. But he needed to walk. He waited only a second for the car to pass, then jogged across to the other side and resumed his march, more determined than ever to find a way to make the obtuse woman appreciate that he was doing as much as he could for her.

'Come on, gorgeous. Spill the beans.' Lydia was sitting sideways in the back seat of the car, her seat belt stretched across her angled frame.

'About what?'

'About that whole weird and wonderful lunch, that's what. I was all ready to impress the socks off the sister in case you were still on audition or something and then in *he* comes in his three piece suit, and onyx cuff-links, all sophisticated and debonair and…I have stop for a moment and just say, yummy…'

Lydia paused to let this new assertion resonate for a moment until she seemed happy that her point had been made.

'To paraphrase, in comes the supreme Mr Lincoln. Then he sits across from you and he changes; he sort of melts as the look he gives you is all adorable and schmaltzy, like he'd prefer to be sitting on your side of the table just so he can look at you up close and personal.'

'Please!' Holly interjected, her cheeks fast burning up.

'I was there. I saw. And I also see you aren't wearing your lucky suit.'

'My what?'

'Whenever we meet with a new client you wear the charcoal trouser suit with the white sleeveless shirt with the plunging neckline and the sexy frill. But not today. Today you're suddenly going out of routine and wearing this dreamy new number.'

Lydia motioned to Holly's impeccable cream calf-length, fitted, square-necked dress.

'It is neither dreamy nor new,' Holly replied truthfully, but she knew that she had taken a great deal of care choosing what to wear to the lunch. 'And I did not know *he* was going to even be there today.'

'But you were going to meet his sister. And who would you more need to make a good first impression on than the sister? It all fits. The goo-goo eyes you two kept shooting at each other were so telling. So spill!'

'He attended my Hidden Valley day as well as the Arty Pants evening, liked them, then offered me the job.' Close enough anyway. 'He's a client, that's it.'

'Not if the divine Mr Lincoln has anything to say in the matter. You've got him hooked. Reel him in and be done with it.'

Lydia was such a dreamer, looking for romance in every chance encounter any time of the day or night. She simply had no idea what sort of person Jacob Lincoln was. She had not been there the other night to see the colour drain from his face at the thought of marriage. Goo-goo eyes or no goo-goo eyes, he was a hopeless case. No strings. No complications. No way.

CHAPTER ELEVEN

HOLLY spent Wednesday at the press junket for a new opera, which would be hitting town in the coming Spring. Thursday she managed the dressing of a debutante ball venue, which she then attended that same night. Alone. Stag. *Sans* date.

What with the party looming, she told Ben, she really did not have time to concentrate on her personal project. In a couple of weeks she would be back on track, but for now all dates were suspended. Suspended indefinitely if that meant landing the Lincoln Holdings account? Perhaps. She hadn't yet given herself the luxury of making that decision.

So in between more imminent projects Holly and Lydia had prepared a detailed preliminary plan for Anabella's party, and they knew it was going to be the best shindig they had ever thrown. But in order for this to be the best shindig they had ever thrown, the client had to be one hundred percent behind them and she knew she could not go any further without that surety. So last thing Friday afternoon Holly called Jacob.

'Holly! I'm surprised to hear from you—pleasantly surprised, of course.' His voice was loud and muffled as he was obviously talking on his car phone. 'What can I do for you?'

'The thing is I really do feel that I should show you our initial plans for the party. You know Anabella, and all I know is she likes pink paper. It'll only take a few minutes, I promise.'

'Sure. How about tonight?'

Holly looked at her watch. But she had no set plans and knew she should really strike before he changed his mind.

'Great.'

'Will Lydia be tagging along or will it be just you?'

'Just me, I'm afraid. Lydia's off to try out some new dance club in the city. The stamina of that girl constantly amazes me.'

'Then how about my place? I'm on my way there now.' She could hear the smile in his voice and it took all of her concentration not to picture him doing so.

'No, I don't think—'

'Why not? I'll cook. It's my turn.'

'There's no need for that. It will only take a minute.' Holly bit her thumbnail. 'Where do you live?'

'Port Melbourne.' He gave the address. On the water's edge and only a few minutes drive from work. She looked around her office. Fabric samples, menus and brochures swamped every spare surface. Quick decision, to stay late on a Friday night and clean up a week's worth of mess or—?

'Okay. How about I pop around in about half an hour? But please don't cook. I'll be out of your hair in time for the evening news, I promise.'

'I'll see you in half an hour, then,' was Jacob's only guarantee.

'Well, there you go,' Jacob said aloud as he hung up.

The excitement in Holly's voice when talking of the party had been palpable. He had wanted to give her something to focus on other than her unreasonable husband hunt and it seemed this party had done the trick.

But why invite her over to your place? How does that

help? Having her alone, at night, in your home, your private sanctuary?

No worries. It would be fine. This night would simply be the passing of the torch to their new professional relationship. And once that was established, they would be on stable ground. She would be happy professionally and he would be free and clear of any obligation he might have felt considering his part in her quest.

Okay, if it's a business meeting we should have an agenda. Much easier to stay in control of the situation if it's mapped out beforehand. First let her get comfortable with you as a business associate, second go over her presentation, and third send her home with the energy and high spirits to complete the project satisfactorily.

If dinner is involved, that's fine too. And maybe a bottle of wine. It will be business, not personal. All to ease the transition, of course.

He put his car in gear and barely kept under the speed limit all the way home.

Holly hurried into her office bathroom to grab a glass of water and caught sight of herself in the floor-length mirror. She was wearing her 'lucky suit', as Lydia called it, and was glad Lydia was not there to ask if it meant she was feeling lucky. And Beth would have a conniption fit at such a time, professing all sorts of fortuitous signs from her choosing that outfit on that day.

'It's nice and it's comfortable,' Holly said aloud to her reflection. 'Besides, tonight is just a presentation like you have done a hundred times before. Choosing to wear a particular outfit hardly portents anything out of the ordinary.'

She smoothed down the neat charcoal pinstripe trouser suit, and soft white sleeveless shirt with its plunging neckline. She ran her fingers through her hair, which for once she was wearing long and loose.

Blissfully ignoring her messy office, she popped the presentation in her 'magic' briefcase, hoping the information inside would work its magic that night, and headed out.

Walking along Lonsdale Street to where her car was parked, she passed the spot where she had first run into Jacob. A flash of intense eyes, mussed hair, hordes of luggage.

She had told Lydia that she had been head down, thinking of work that morning. But the truth was she had seen him exit his hotel. She had *watched* him, arms full of luggage, chill wind whipping his hair about his face, beckoning the hotel doorman to remain inside, insisting he stay out of the cold.

He had been so handsome, huffing and puffing in exertion as he had navigated his way, unassisted, to the kerb. And she had been smitten.

Holly slowed as she passed the hotel, the memory of him dragging his tired eyes from the bustling traffic to glance in her direction sending a delightful shiver along her spine.

He had not let go of his cumbersome cases, or stopped heading to the edge of the road, but from that moment he had only had eyes for her. And that look, both exhausted and vibrant, along with its accompanying hint of a smile, had almost frozen her to the spot. Only the biting cold and primal need to get inside to warmth had kept her legs moving. He'd watched her with such unconcealed interest, though her extremities had frozen, her insides had melted. Her pulse had quickened, and she'd barely been able to focus from the blood pumping so hard and fast through her head.

She'd had no choice; she'd had to pass him to get to

her office, the front door of which had been barely a block behind him. She had walked on, unsteady but determined, her knees shaking as she'd walked closer and closer, her breathing ragged, unable to drag her eyes away from the stranger in her sights. Then—

Bam!

How they had come to collide, she had no idea. They had both been walking towards one another, eyes locked, and in those last few seconds should have tacitly agreed to walk to one side, allowing the other to pass. But somewhere during those last few seconds, neither had been able to do as politeness dictated.

Mightily embarrassed at having found herself sprawled at his feet, and at the fact that she had been devouring him with her eyes only moments before, she had lashed out, and the exquisite spell that had woven its way around her heart had been shattered.

Having passed the hotel and rounded the corner, Holly shook off the disturbing memory. It was not at all productive thinking about it, not for their business relationship, nor if she had any serious hope of eventually finding someone else, someone compatible to spend her life with. No point daydreaming about someone so unsuitable and unattainable.

It was time she heeded her own advice to Jacob, and *pretended it never happened.*

Twenty minutes later Holly stood outside a large five-storey apartment building in Port Melbourne. She pressed the intercom button for the penthouse, no less.

The street was bustling with young people rugged up in overcoats on their way to pubs and popular restaurants along the water's edge. A fair way down a long jetty, the cruise ship the *Spirit of Tasmania* waited silently to take her human cargo on her nightly trek across Bass Strait.

After about a minute, Jacob's voice answered, 'Holly?'

'Yep.' Her teeth chattered from standing in the biting cold.

'Come on up.'

The door buzzed and Holly scampered inside, thankful to be warmed by central heating once more.

She approached the security guard at the desk and he checked her name against a list before pointing the way to the lifts.

As she rode the lift to the top floor Holly prepared herself for a glimpse into Jacob's private world. If a man's home was his refuge, she craved to see what Jacob's home would divulge. Floor five lit up and the doors opened. The sweet fragrance of soy sauce and honey and tremulous strains of jazz music wafted into her cubicle.

Holly had thought her own home attractive and quite substantial, but this was something else. Jacob's home was neither stark and intimidating, nor overtly manly. Instead, with its open-plan, blonde polished wood floors, strategic ambient lighting and elegant neutral furniture it was tasteful and welcoming.

A stainless steel kitchen took up the right side of the huge room. A three-piece lounge suite filled the left side facing a fireplace, above which two oversized abstract prints of American jazz singers held pride of place. A shiny golden trumpet was the only item adorning the mantel.

On a raised platform at the far end sat the dining suite. The entire far wall was comprised of ceiling-to-floor tinted windows. The multicoloured twinkling lights of the city skyline and the glow of the fast-setting sun shone through the extra-thick smoky-grey glass producing a mercurial spectacular view.

She called out, 'Hello? Anyone home?'

Jacob poked his head out of a hidden doorway on the far side of the kitchen. 'Grab a drink from the bar in the kitchen. I'll be with you in a sec.'

His head disappeared again.

On the kitchen bench Holly found Jacob's tray of spirits lined up with a crystal decanter and crystal glasses. Ignoring the offer, she discarded her briefcase on the floor next to the bench and did a turn about the room.

She ran her hand across the back of the soft cream lounge, scanned the titles of the numerous books lining the long hip-high bookshelves that separated the dining room from the lounge. She walked up the three steps to the raised level and marvelled at the city lights reflecting off the glass-topped dining table. She could feel the cool of the coming night radiating through the thick glass of the window. She moved to stand so close her breath formed on the window.

'You like?'

Holly turned with her hand at her heart as Jacob's soft voice scared her out of her reverie. She had not even heard him come up behind her.

He handed her a glass of red wine and she took a quick sip. Peeking over the top of her wineglass, she noticed his hair was still damp as evidenced by the smooth comb lines running through it. And even through the intoxicating aroma of the heavy red wine she could smell mint. Toothpaste? Then she remembered seeing a few faint shiny patches on the floor on her way in. It suddenly registered that the patches were in fact wet footprints and that she must have caught him in the shower.

She turned back towards the window, hoping he had not noticed her blush. 'How could anyone not like it? Your apartment is lovely, Jacob. And the view is breathtaking.' She swept a hand in front of her, encompassing the entire panorama.

'This was the first residential property I bought,' Jacob said.

'You own the building?' Holly asked, spinning back to face him, her intrigue overcoming her embarrassment. *Marble floors, a security guard, city views. Phew.*

'I did. I financed its refurbishment several years ago and then sold it off piece by piece, keeping the best apartment for myself. Admittedly I made no money on the deal, I came out even for the first, and hopefully last, time, but I think the sacrifice was worth it.'

'Indeed.'

'Every time I come back it makes me wonder why I ever chose to leave.'

Holly took another sip of the delicious wine, entranced by the city lights reflected in Jacob's eyes and unable to swallow down an unreasonable hope that he would never leave again. As though sensing the acute emotion she could not contain, Jacob took a small step forward, bringing them to within a foot of each other.

She felt a torrid tingling sensation well up in her feet as all of the blood seemed to have ventured further north.

The cool perfumes of mint and now shampoo fought for her attention. With them came jumbled scented memories of fresh rain.

She watched Jacob's hand leave his glass and slowly, slowly ease its way towards her. Her breath caught in her throat. Her hands felt slippery and warm as she clutched the glass to her chest.

Her eyes closed, too heavy with expectation to remain open any longer, and she waited, unable and unwilling to prevent whatever was about to happen.

CHAPTER TWELVE

AND then the music stopped. The jazz CD had finished. With a slight cough Jacob stepped that same small step back to his original position.

This movement snapped Holly out of her trance and after blinking rapidly several times she too moved, willing her numb legs to step smartly around him and down the steps towards the kitchen.

'I have the presentation in my bag,' she prattled as she moved further and further from the window, and from Jacob, her heels clacking on the polished wood floor, the noise comfortingly louder than the beating of her heart. 'Maybe we should sit on the couch and I'll go through it with you quickly so I can get out of your hair.'

She placed the half-empty glass on the kitchen bench and reached down to grab her briefcase.

Jacob had moved down to the bookshelves and was re-starting the CD in the discreetly concealed stereo. As the soft strains of the mellow song wafted from numerous hidden speakers around the apartment Jacob turned to face her.

Holly stood, rooted to the spot. The moment was upon her. This was what she had so keenly wished to see. The man in his environment.

The reality was a man a couple of inches over six feet, with thick springy dark hair, rich hazel eyes frayed by long, dark lashes. A man whose slightly crooked smile could turn her knees to butter and whose occasional dimples made her lose her focus and resolve every time they surfaced. A man wearing velvety soft chocolate-brown trousers, a lightweight sweater, which emphasized the width of his shoulders and the well-developed muscles beneath, a silver and gold two-tone sports watch, no rings or other jewellery. A man content to spend a Friday night at home on a comfortable couch, sipping on a good red wine and listening to lazy jazz music.

Jacob walked towards her and she saw that he was also a man wearing no shoes. *So that's how he crept up on me so quietly,* Holly thought as her eyes snapped back up to his. The cheeky look in his eyes dared her to accuse him of anything.

As he approached her she stood her ground, her briefcase held like armour in front of her. Once at her side he leaned towards her. Her breath caught in her throat and she could not move. Then at the last second his hand reached out, grabbing her red wine glass from the kitchen bench top. Then just as casually he turned and strolled towards the lounge. He had not come within a foot of her yet she was shaking from his proximity.

'Are you coming?' he called over his shoulder.

Holly released the deep breath she had been holding, gathered her wits then walked over to join him. He had lounged on one of the long four-seater couches in his usual idle manner and she joined him there, though far enough away that their knees had no chance of touching.

'What important details have you got to show me?' Jacob asked, amusement lacing every word.

Holly glared at him. 'You may not think this meeting will be valuable, but if it means that Anabella's party is the better for it then why object?'

Rather than be offended, he looked at her with respect, as he always seemed to when she stood up to him. 'Go ahead, then. Though I must say I never once said your coming here would prove invaluable.'

'Yes, well, good, then,' she stammered as she collected her thoughts. But once she clapped eyes back on her party notes, her confidence returned. This she could do in her sleep.

She went through every detail regarding venue, catering and décor, leaving not a single suggestion out. She finished her presentation with the fact she had chosen a luxurious banquet hall owned by Lincoln Holdings, as she already knew he preferred to use his own establishments for his events. When Jacob did not respond she looked up to find his eyes spectacularly crossed.

'What was that for?'

He uncrossed his eyes and grinned. 'First things first, Holly—you do realise that I am a man?'

She had not met a man more obviously masculine. 'For the sake of argument, yes.'

'Well, then, you must understand that I find words such as "georgette" and *"decoupage"* mind-boggling.'

Holly went to interrupt but Jacob held a finger to her lips, shutting her up quick smart.

'Believe me, I am not diminishing what you do, I hired you because I admit you can do it better. If you came here for my approval, then you have it. Book everything. Hire everybody. Just go right ahead. But first things first, stay right where you are.'

He quickly pulled his finger from her mouth, kissed it and placed it back on her lips before bounding out of the chair and jogging into the kitchen.

'Now, I have to give this a quick stir and add the veggies for half a second and then I will be able to blind you with my culinary talents.'

'Oh, no,' Holly said, shoving her bits and pieces quickly

into her briefcase, fighting the urge to vigorously rub away the warm impression his finger had left on her lips. 'I thought I made it clear I wasn't staying for dinner.'

As she passed by the kitchen her nostrils were filled with that same delicious soy and honey aroma she had smelled earlier. Her stomach grumbled and she placed her hand over it to quell the noise, hoping Jacob had not heard.

'Do you have dinner plans already?' he asked. *Another hot date with a potential husband,* was left unsaid, but it echoed clearly enough in the air between them.

Holly opened her mouth to answer and in the moment during which she should have come up with a believable lie, she wavered, picturing her dark, empty apartment and the leftover tuna casserole she was planning to reheat.

Still she was about to decline when she caught the look on Jacob's face. Though he was acting cool, aloof, indifferent, he was obviously sweating on her answer. His lips had thinned, pressed together too tightly, he was stirring the dinner ingredients more vigorously than seemed necessary and he kept shooting her short, accusatory sideways glances. If she hadn't known him better she would have thought him jealous.

After several moments of telling silence, Jacob's shoulders relaxed, his thinned lips softened into his usual crooked, beguiling smile and she knew he had caught her hesitation loud and clear.

'Good,' he said. 'So stay.' He added the vegetables to the mix with a deft hand.

He seemed so relaxed. As if he had flipped a lever and they had gone from God knew what to business associates in the blink of an eye. Maybe he could turn his nature on and off like that but Holly was not so fortunate.

'Don't you find this in the least bit uncomfortable?'

'What's that?'

'That you know about my future plans and desires. I find it uncomfortable enough to face you as a friend of a friend, much less as a prospective client.'

That earned her another of his unreadable glances. 'I understand what you think you mean,' he said, 'but I just don't believe you.'

'Excuse me?'

He paused, stopped stirring and stared. 'The truth is I like you, Holly.'

Holly gripped her briefcase tight, clinging to it, feeling as though if she let go it would rise to the ceiling like a dozen helium balloons and take her with it.

He paused a moment to taste the stir-fry and, obviously finding it satisfactory, he finished his thoughts.

'My closest friends are your closest friends. My business and your business will be of great benefit to each other. So what if I know that your current goal is hooking a husband and I am still willing to have you over to my place on a dinner date? Maybe one thing does not have to exclude the other.'

Holly's knees all but buckled beneath her.

So much for his agenda. So much for it's business not personal. Who was he kidding?

She was one big spanner in the works of any agenda he could ever hope to follow. Standing there, her glorious hair spilling over her shoulders, her huge eyes pleading for him to put her out of her misery, one way or the other. It was all he could do not to just haul her off to his bedroom like some caveman and show her exactly how uncomfortable she made him feel. He didn't know what they were. But they were no more 'friends of friends' than they were business associates.

He should change his mind. Thank her for her thorough

presentation and send her home. But the words that came out of his mouth were, 'It's not complicated. Let's stop avoiding each other when we could be having so much more fun enjoying each other. At least until the thing you most wish for becomes more imminent anyway.'

There. Now how's that for a spanner in the works?

Jacob wiped his hands on a clean teatowel, poured two new glasses of wine and grabbed two rolled-up napkins from the kitchen bench. He passed her on his way to the dining table, the determined look in his eyes daring her to disagree with his perfectly sensible proposal.

What thing? Holly wondered, the idea of she and Jacob 'enjoying each other' pretty much blotting out the rest of his speech.

Oh, a husband. A partner. Someone to love you. Someone like Jacob.

And like a bolt of lightning it hit her. Right in the stomach. Like a sucker punch. And she was lucky not to have collapsed under its weight.

Talk about complicating things. She was head over heels for Jacob.

Ever since she had seen him dragging his heavy luggage along the footpath, she had been lost. She had been filled with a longing, which she had mistakenly tried to shoulder onto someone else, anyone else, other than the one who had produced it in the first place. She knew without any doubt her husband hunt had been over from the moment it began.

He lay the glasses on the table, unrolled the linen napkins, which contained two sets of cutlery, and shifted a small vase of wildflowers so they would not hamper their view of one another across the table. Every move appeared to her in slow motion.

It cannot possibly be love, she thought. *I barely know him. But you can know someone for ever and not love them, so why can't the opposite be possible?* And the unremitting feeling of weightlessness since he'd admitted to merely liking her was like nothing she had ever felt before.

But he's not the marrying kind and has said as much from day one.

Remember?

And the whole perfect-husband theory meant you were not to fall for a guy like him. A guy who was self-important, shallow and self-serving.

Remember?

But she could not remember how she could ever have thought those things about Jacob. The man whistling melodiously along with the lovely music was confident, to be sure. But more than that he was protective and generous, kind and considerate. He was also barefoot and cooking up a storm. For her.

The stir-fry sizzled enthusiastically and Jacob jogged back to the kitchen and turned off the stove. He grabbed two dinner plates, onto which he heaped generous portions of the delicious-looking dinner.

'No more excuses, okay,' Jacob said.

Holly did her best to compose her features to appear the same as she had looked before her alarming revelation.

'I have cooked enough of this lip-smacking dinner for the both of us. You have no other dinner plans. You are here already. You are able-bodied enough to grab the bottle of wine and bring it to the table. Put down that heavy briefcase and come give me a hand.'

Okay, Holly thought, knowing something had switched inside of her and she was going to have a hell of a time switching back. *Whatever you say.*

CHAPTER THIRTEEN

HOLLY finished off the last morsel on her plate. She had long since discarded her suit jacket. But even in just her filmy frilly top, in the fire-lit room she was warm and cosy.

'That was heavenly,' Holly said, patting the napkin to the sides of her mouth and then placing it on the table.

'Hmm. Heavenly,' Jacob agreed.

Watching Jacob sitting back, his hands clasped across his stomach, a contented smile lighting his lovely face, it was too easy for Holly to let herself believe he was thinking the same thing she was. That it was heavenly enough just to be sitting there together.

'Where did you learn to cook like that?'

Jacob reached for his wine. His eyes seemed to narrow briefly as he took a determined gulp, but after swallowing the mouthful he answered her. 'I moved out of home when I was sixteen so if I wanted to eat more than tinned soup and toast I had to learn how to cook.'

'Sixteen, really? Were you young and rash and ready to take on the world?'

'It was more that I was determined to become somebody, to make money and keep it, and to never want for anything.'

'My biggest ambition at that age was to drive my dad crazy by running off to marry Toby Cox, the cutest boy in my class.'

'I guess some things never change.'

Holly blushed. As the corners of Jacob's mouth twitched

in the hint of a smile she had a glimpse of the dimples, and it was worth every trace of embarrassment.

'Did your drive come from your parents, do you think?' she asked. 'They usually provoke fairly strong responses from kids of that age.'

'My strong response was that I did not want to end up like them. Well, not like my father, to be more precise.'

'Tell me more.' *Tell me everything.* Holly leaned forward with her chin on her palm, intrigued, and waited until he was ready to go on.

'By the time I was a teenager, more of his money was going on surreptitious boozing than paying the bills. Once I caught my poor mother searching Dad's jacket pockets for loose change in order to pay the milkman. And when she died, he barely left the house, and then only to head down to the local pub. So the day after my sixteenth birthday I left.'

'I had no idea, Jacob. I didn't mean to pry—'

'It's okay. I've never hidden my modest beginnings. In fact, it has been fairly well documented. "Poor boy makes good" is always a better headline than "Rich kid is still rich".'

Holly glanced at Jacob's half drunk glass of wine. 'Was he an alcoholic?'

Jacob smiled ruefully at his glass, gently swirling the contents.

'Possibly. Though I have always thought him more weak-willed than having an addictive personality. Being drunk was an excuse not to make a decision.'

'And you have based your life around not being like that?'

'Absolutely. It was the perfect example of failing to take life by the horns. I find no point in being tied down in one project. Take the risk, reap the rewards, and move on to the next venture.'

He sounded so earnest. But to Holly it felt as if he had said this same speech a thousand times in his head. And it broke her heart. She had known a man who had lived by that maxim and all it had done was hurt those who loved him most.

'And Anabella?' Holly asked, her voice soft. 'She's younger than you?'

Jacob dropped his intense gaze to the table, but not before Holly was certain she saw a wave of guilt pass over his absorbing hazel eyes.

'She was only twelve at the time. We wrote to each other a bit and she let on she wasn't happy, but at the time I figured it was more important for me to make money so that later she would be set.'

Jacob absently took a large gulp of wine.

'A few years later I came home, a man of means and experience, rid of my resentment towards my father. Or so I thought. I walked in to find half of the furniture gone, a pile of ironing covering the couch and Ana practically tied to the sink. She was only four years older but had aged so that I barely recognised her. Her clothes were ragged, and her hair had been chopped short, by her own hand, I later discovered. My bright, beautiful little sister was all but gone, replaced with this listless, miserable creature.'

'Jacob,' Holly whispered. She lifted a finger to cover her trembling lips, blinking fast to clear the tears blurring her vision. *What have I begun?*

Why did I begin? Jacob asked himself.

But he was unable to drag his eyes away from Holly's compassionate face. *When she looked at me with those big blue eyes and asked such a simple question, about cooking, what made me leap into this tale?*

It was like leaping off a bridge but all it had taken was for her to ask, and he had leapt. He felt as if he were dangling over the edge and that Holly had control of the only rope that could bring him back to safety. Yet he had complete faith that she would not let go.

And now he had started he knew there was no way he could stop until the whole thing played itself out.

'Angered beyond thought, and before I even had the chance to hug the poor girl, I forced her to tell me where *he* was. Down at the local pub, of course. I found him sitting at the bar, a frail shell of the man I had once known. I tossed him the papers to our family home. I had paid off his mortgage. He glanced at the papers, barely registering the fact of them, much less the enormous symbolic gesture of reconciliation I had offered him. I left in disgust, went home, collected Ana and left without a note, knowing that at least now he could wallow in his own self-misery with a roof over his head but without taking Ana down with him.'

'So you looked after her?'

Jacob nodded.

'But you were only twenty.'

'I know, but what choice did we have? So the next few years I was her rock, her whole life, until she managed to get back on her feet.' *I don't ever want to feel that exposed again. Having someone else depend so entirely on me. It was just so hard.*

Holly nodded. And Jacob felt sure it was not just an affectation. She had heard the unsaid words and she understood.

'What happened to your father?'

Jacob shrugged. 'He passed away about four years ago.'

'Before you left for New Orleans?'

Jacob inhaled sharply. *She doesn't miss a beat.*

'That week. After the funeral I made the move.' *Took off, more like it.*

'It all seems to have turned out for the best, don't you think? You've certainly done well for yourself and you and Anabella are on good terms.'

'But Ana has been spoilt,' he said. 'She's never been interested in holding down a job, and would rather burn her clothes than wash and iron them herself. And that's my failing.'

Holly had found out what she wanted to know. Her lovely Jacob had exhausted more emotions in the last years of his childhood than most people did in a lifetime. Then in adulthood decided if he had no feelings, they could never consume him.

How could she hope to bring someone back from that sort of pain? She had hardly experienced the kind of rich, fulfilled childhood and stable family that could make it all better for him.

But she would do her best to try.

'Jacob. Are you kidding me? You helped a child become an adult. Many people never get that chance.'

'I was clueless.'

'You were a kid. You can hardly have been expected to know all the answers.'

Jacob shifted in his chair, trying to throw off the strange feeling that had fast crept up on him. He found himself reaching for Holly's reassurance. And that was exactly what he had just finished telling himself he never wanted to endure again.

He felt that familiar old need to just run and run. But this time he would not look back.

And then Holly took his palm in hers.

'Listen to me.'

What choice did he have as she stroked the back of his hand? He listened.

'From what Beth has told me of Ana, she is compassionate and optimistic, serious and spirited. Without her specific blend of life experiences she may not have taken on that formidable combination of traits.'

His hand tingled from the inadvertent patterns she was weaving across his skin. 'You are probably right.'

'No probably about it, I am right. I truly believe a person needs highs and lows, comedy and tragedy in order to mature into a valuable, well-rounded personality. I mean, without the sad times how can you really enjoy the happy times? You know how it feels so good after a great big sneeze?'

Jacob was completely caught off guard. The corners of his mouth twitched in the beginnings of a smile. 'Sure.'

'Well, that's because of the intense discomfort and irritation preceding it. You know how it goes. That first slight tingle that makes your nose twitch, which then grows into that bothersome tickle that builds and builds into an exasperating itch. And then comes the sneeze and when it is released, ahhh, what a wonderful sensation. But that wonderful sensation is only the same non-sensation you had before the tingle even started. Basically the good feeling only exists because of the bad feeling prior to it.'

Jacob's laughter came more easily. 'I guess there is some peculiar sense in there somewhere.'

'Peculiar or not, it's true. Without understanding of deep sorrow there can be no appreciation of sheer joy.'

Holly patted him companionably on the hand, pushed

her chair back and stood up. 'Now, my friend, could you please point the way to the little girls' room?'

Jacob pointed down the stairs to the doorway next to the kitchen. Holly smiled her thanks and rubbed Jacob's shoulder as she passed him by, sending a wash of warmth from her lithe fingertips through his tense shoulder.

As she reached the door she turned back for a moment, as though she knew he was studying her, and smiled before disappearing into the room beyond.

A small smile played at Jacob's lips as he thought of his younger sister and her love of stray animals, her abhorrence of reality television and refusal to cut her long dark hair any shorter than her shoulder blades. Without those traits and without his support through those formative years, she would not be the same Ana.

With a deep, contented sigh, Jacob rose from his seat and cleared the table, whistling softly along with the upbeat jazz music as he did, a spring in his step and a serenity he did not remember *ever* feeling.

As Holly washed her hands in the bathroom sink she looked into the mirror. Her lipstick was all but gone; only a light burgundy stain remained on her full lips. Her tongue ran over her teeth, once again tasting the honey soy stir-fry Jacob had cooked.

In the corner of the mirror she caught sight of a bath, which was so huge it took up all of one corner of the spacious room. It was certainly large enough to fit Jacob's tall frame. Easily. As well as that of another person.

Her eyes swung back to the mirror so she faced herself head-on.

'Holly, get a grip,' she growled through clenched teeth. 'And get your briefcase and get out of here before you do something you can't take back.' *Something worse than just picturing him stripping off and lowering his long, muscular length into a hot bath filled with bubbles...*

'Holly!' she said aloud, bringing her hands to her face and slapping herself lightly. She had to shake off the growing ardour that mental picture had initiated.

Jacob was a guy who needed time and space. He needed patience and kind words. She felt as though he had made some progress out there tonight and the last thing he needed was some husband-hungry woman leaping into his arms and professing her undying love.

Once free of the bathroom, Holly found herself back in what she assumed was Jacob's bedroom.

The natural tones and unpretentious feel of the room matched the rest of the home. 'St John's ace lithograph' filled an otherwise blank wall above the bed head and bookshelves ran the length of one wall.

This could be her one and only time there and she could not resist soaking up as much of Jacob's habitat as possible. She ran her fingers along the smooth, clean horizontal planes of the bookshelves. Amongst the numerous books there sat a few photo frames; most housed pictures of Jacob with a thin brunette woman. Holly ran a finger over the girl's face, assuming it was Anabella. She had the same dark hair and deep hazel eyes and her smile towards her brother was bursting with love.

And between a pair of stout candleholders and a bunch of unused candles sat a pair of much-used boxing gloves in a glass case.

She stopped short at this last item, staring at the rough, rounded surfaces with their numerous cracks, bruises and stains. Looking closer, she even thought she could make out splatters of dried blood on the knuckle of the right hand. A chill ran down her spine as her mind clouded with a flash of images of how those marks and scrapes would have been achieved. She knew exactly what it took for a pair of well-worn boxing gloves to look like that.

Then she remembered that Jacob was the man who had organised those dangerous boxing bouts for his employees to 'enjoy'. She found it hard reconciling her memory of the antagonistic, commanding, condescending man of that night with the astute, intriguing, reflective man on the other side of the door.

But they were one and the same.

Jacob, whom Ben and Beth considered a close and worthy friend, who worried for his little sister, and who had unsuspectingly captured Holly's heart was the same ruthless and unfettered Jacob Lincoln of Lincoln Holdings.

The clink of china from the dining room jolted Holly from her puzzled reverie. Having no idea how long she had been snooping, she decided it was time to leave.

On her way to the door she passed a chest of drawers. Her mind reeling to a conversation she'd had with Beth a few days before, Holly turned back and opened the top drawer. She stared at the contents for a long moment before shutting the drawer quietly.

'Definitely time to go home,' she whispered aloud as she walked out of the room.

CHAPTER FOURTEEN

HOLLY walked into the main room determined to find her host so that she could make her excuses and leave. The table had been cleared and cleaned but there was no sign of Jacob. She moved to the hearth to wait for him to return. Her skin tingled from a mixture of the sizzling heat of the fire and a whole different warmth that had lit her from within since she'd come to realise that she was in love.

She caught sight of something hidden in a shadowy corner, and moved in that direction for a closer look, when the lights in that corner sprang on in a blinding flash.

Holly screamed as she spun around, her eyes searching wildly for Jacob. He was near the front doorway, his hands moving down from a bank of light switches on the wall by his shoulder.

'Sorry,' he said as he sauntered towards her. All signs of the reclusive man from dinner had vanished and he was replaced with a Jacob she had not seen before. The approving warmth in his eyes was so unmistakable, for the first time she felt like she was the hunted.

'I didn't mean to startle you,' he said, his voice low and husky. 'I knew you were heading to my bag so I thought I'd make it easier for you to have a nose around.'

'Your bag?' Holly asked, her voice barely above a whisper.

Jacob held out his arm motioning her towards the corner. She turned back to see a red punching bag hanging there sedately.

She swallowed hard. It was colossal. Taller than her by

half. Thick metallic chains ran from both ends, connecting the bag to large matching steel plates bolted to the floor and ceiling.

Taking the last few steps towards the bag, she reached out tentatively and gave it a slight push. The heavy bag barely moved. She pulled her hand away as thought burnt by the touch, rubbing her fingers together committing to memory the rough, cool feel of the worn leather.

Jacob joined her, his hands on hips and his eyes bright. 'When I refurbished the place I had the roof and floor reinforced so as to take its weight. Do you want a go?'

He slapped the bag playfully a couple of times. Holly baulked, her pulse quickening in loathing at the thought. She backed away holding up her hands defensively.

'No, thank you.'

'Are you sure? It's great fun.'

'Sorry. I have no interest in beating up a big red bag that has never done anything to deserve my wrath.'

'It's good for releasing tension. And it's excellent exercise. It'll work muscles you never knew you had,' Jacob promised as he jogged up and down with loose fists raised at the big bag.

Holly kept walking backwards, putting herself as far from the bag and Jacob's flailing fists as possible. 'If I hadn't discovered those muscles to date I'm sure I can get through the next fifty years without them.' She kept her voice light, to stop herself sounding as she felt. Frantic. 'And aren't there better ways to release tension than hitting something or someone?'

'I can think of at least one.'

Holly stopped short. Her eyes flew to Jacob's and she was all but undone.

He had stopped bouncing around. His feet were shoulder-width apart, and he had steadied the heavy bag in two hands. His dark soft hair was tousled from the exercise and a lock flopped down his forehead. His eyes were bright and his breathing was heavy.

If her mind had not already been conjuring up inappropriate sensual images, she would have taken that as a serious invitation. And what an invitation that could have been. The man before her was so male, so virile it was enough to wrench any woman's heart. Add to that the 'nobody can touch my heart' aura he carried with him like a weight across his broad shoulders and he was an irresistible package.

But the fact that he had long since had Holly's for the taking meant she was in danger of seeing meaning in his looks and words that were not there. She could almost convince herself she saw her own desire reflected in his bright hazel eyes.

What a picture she makes, Jacob thought. Her blue eyes flashed and her own heavy breathing was more than a match for his. For someone he once thought cool and calm, she was the most emotive woman he had ever met. Every thought and fancy played across her face the second it crossed her mind. And if she wasn't careful, he would take the three steps over there and make good her very thoughts and fancies.

He had thrown the line out in jest. Sort of. But instead of a raised eyebrow and a haughty stare he had been hit with a look of undisguised passion. A silent submission. And it shocked him to his core.

What would happen if he made good on that throwaway invitation? What an encounter that could be. If only she were that sort of woman.

If only.

His mind had been spinning in that direction all night.

Who was he kidding? It had been spinning that way for two weeks. And if that look was anything to go by, her mind had been spinning on a similar track.

But this was not a woman to be toyed with. Ben and Beth's best friend. He should never have cooked her dinner. She had been right about that from the outset. There was no point. It was too close to home. It would be too complicated.

But, oh, it would be so sweet.

Jacob ran a hand through his hair, took a step away from the bag. Time to wipe that mesmerising look from her lovely face. Time to change the subject.

'Do you really have such an objection to boxing or are you just claiming the accepted feminine view for my benefit?'

Holly blinked.

That's better. Dislike me. Fight me.

Then she lifted her chin in defiance.

Better still.

'And what would I be hoping to gain in coming across as acceptably feminine?'

He wanted her up and debating. Much safer than standing before him so quiet, so lovely, making him ache through wanting to touch her. He reached out and took hold of the bag once more, needing to distract himself from his runaway thoughts. Better his hands occupied there than reaching out for her.

'All I'm saying is that I'd rather hear your opinion than an expected opinion any day.'

There, that should get her worked up.

'Truthfully, Jacob, that is my opinion, expected or not,' she said, seeming to drag the statement from deep within her.

Jacob watched in chagrin as the fight drained out of her.

She deflated before his eyes until she looked so sad, so tired, and so vulnerable, as though she had been pretending to be strong for such a long time and could do it no longer. She could not know how it affected him.

'This all frightens me a little.' She motioned to the punching bag. 'The first time we met you yelled at me, a complete stranger in the street, then there was that horrible boxing match at the Fun and Games where you advocated violence to your employees. Then I found those old gloves in what amounts to a shrine in your bedroom, and now this. There seems to be an unsettling pattern forming.'

The one word that had captured Jacob's attention had been the word 'frightens'. Only then did he detect Holly's panicky expression. Her hands were clasped defensively in front of her chest and her feet were planted firmly as though she was ready to fly at any sign of trouble. And she flinched with every random slap he gave the bag.

Jacob moved away from the bag, lightly taking Holly's arm to lead her to sit with him on the big couch by the fire.

'What are you frightened of, Holly?'

She didn't answer, just shrugged and swallowed hard, her big blue eyes wide, still focussed on the bag in the distance. Jacob kept hold of both of her hands in one of his. With his other hand he lightly stroked her hair to relax her and kept his voice deliberately soft.

'Big Red over there is just for fun and fitness. Though as a kid I had a good teacher who took me aside and joined me up for elementary boxing classes at a local gym. It taught me how to master my emotions and how to focus on the task in front of me. I put on matches for the staff to teach them those same ideals.'

'And the gloves?' she asked, her voice subdued and wavering.

'The gloves once belonged to Muhammad Ali and are encased in glass in the safety of my room as they are worth a small fortune.'

Holly seemed to have relaxed very little. Her eyes had softened and lost that startled look, but she still shook. Jacob's hands now stroked her hair from her face, behind her ears, around behind her neck. He still sought to relax her but he was also finding the touch exhilarating and was soon doing it for his own benefit as much as hers.

'It's no big deal, Holly. Really. I mean, Ana has a punching bag at her place. I dare say she uses hers more than I do these days. She loves it. Haven't you ever done kick boxing, or self defence classes?'

'I take yoga with Beth every week,' she answered quietly, and then a hesitant smile lit her lovely face. 'Just plain old yoga, not even power yoga.'

Jacob shifted in his seat. His heart rate rose after just one quick smile from her. Not sensible. He slowly drew his hands away from her, resting one on his thigh and the other along the back of the couch. He had more important things to get from this conversation than the delight of her touch.

'Holly, I haven't been in a fist fight since I was sixteen and have never used my skills outside of a ring. I promise. I have never hit a woman and never would.' He shot her a playful smile. 'No matter how exasperating I know some of them can be.'

But instead of laughing along with him as he had hoped, she flinched and shrank within herself. Did she have to be so sensitive?

Leaning forward, he raised her head with a finger under her chin. 'Come on, Holly, this is ridiculous. I need to know that you believe me. I couldn't endure thinking that you were seriously fearful of me. Tell me you believe me.'

Holly swallowed hard as she looked into his pleading eyes. 'I believe you,' she said.

But Jacob saw the uncertainty. He also saw that this uncertainty was worrying her, as though she really wanted to believe in him. There had to be a significant reason behind this wish to believe and the idea invigorated him.

If she saw him as merely a client with whom she was having a business dinner, or even as a 'friend of a friend', it really shouldn't matter to her. But evidently it did matter. Before he could tell himself it was a bad idea, Jacob leant forward ever so slightly and she did not turn away.

Holly waited silently as Jacob's face came closer and closer to her own, until his lips touched hers, so lightly, just as they had that misty night on Beth and Ben's driveway. And just as readily the kiss turned into something deeper and more exhilarating.

Jacob leaned in a fraction closer, pressing his warm mouth firmly against her own, and Holly turned her head so that their lips met more fully. She was still holding her weight with her palms on either side of her thighs, her elbows locked.

After several moments of blissfully enjoying the sweet taste of Jacob's soft, supple mouth, Holly felt her arms go weak and her elbows unlocked, causing her to sink back ever so slightly. But it was enough. Jacob slid an arm behind her and leaned her back into the plush chair, guiding her, his strong arm taking her weight until she rested comfortably along the seat.

Desire raging through her, she felt his warm imprint

along her receptive body, his heavy male scent making as much of an impression on her awakened senses as his strong insistent body.

Her breathing hastened until she felt as though she would pass out if she were not already lying down. Smooth and skilled, his teeth tugged lightly at her bottom lip, intermittently nipping and pulling away, creating a longing ache deep within her so that she found herself craning to meet his mouth. This was the Jacob she loved. Generous, sweet, intoxicating.

And all too soon, above the heady, insistent ringing of blood in her ears, came the shrill, insistent ring of the telephone.

'Shouldn't you get that?' Holly asked, whispering against Jacob's tender mouth.

As if in punishment for her even noticing the phone, Jacob shifted his attentions from her warm mouth to her ear, softly fanning hot, short breaths at the base of her lobe and raining delicate kisses along her exposed neck.

'The machine will get it.'

And so it did.

'This is Jacob, leave a message.'

'Hiya bro.' Anabella's cheerful voice came over the machine.

Holly placed her hands firmly on Jacob's chest; both of their faces turned towards the phone, though only an inch apart.

'The snow's fast and furious and so is the skiing. And no, I haven't broken a leg. Mikey says hi. How's the party coming along? Did you meet up with Holly as you promised? If she's as lovely as you say maybe you should ask her out. Sorry, I can't help it. When I'm in love I have to share it around. Anyway, let me know how it's going and I'll see you in a week. Love ya.'

The phone clicked as she hung up and the machine went through the beeps and whirrs necessary to reset itself.

Her senses slowly returning, Holly did not wait for Jacob to turn his face back to hers. She pushed at his chest to lift him and he conceded.

'I take it that was Ana.' She swung her legs back onto the floor.

'Mmm hmm,' Jacob answered, his eyes not leaving her. One of his hands rested lightly on her thigh and the other curled in and out of a lock of her hair.

'Look, I really should go.' If she didn't she could so easily fall under the spell of that strong hand and those mesmerising lips once more. All too easily. She should not have given into that sensational bliss in the first place. But how could she not? Though next time her common sense was unlikely to be saved by the phone.

'Why?' Jacob asked.

Why? Holly thought. *Because I am at once enamoured and afraid of you and at real risk of leaping into your arms and not letting go thus of making a complete fool of myself and sending you running for the hills.*

'I really had no intention of even staying for dinner and then afterwards…' She could not find the words to explain what had happened afterwards. 'This isn't what I expected.'

Jacob smiled. 'Let's just agree it has been a most unexpected evening on every count. In fact we seem to only ever have unexpected times together. I certainly couldn't call our encounters predictable.'

How easily he can joke. He really has no idea. Holly

knew she should be glad. At least that way she could hopefully extricate herself from her own feelings without anyone ever knowing.

But she wasn't glad. She was frustrated. He was attracted to her, that much was obvious. But that much was
as far as it went for him. And it wasn't enough. Not now.
Not when she knew how she really felt about him.

Holly smiled shortly before easing herself away from
Jacob's light touch, standing up and meticulously straight-
ening her clothes. She looked around, not quite knowing
where to turn next until Jacob stood and motioned to her
briefcase by the kitchen.

'Right, of course. Thank you,' Holly said. She collected
her jacket and bag, and headed straight for the lift. She
pressed the button and turned to face Jacob who was standing only a couple of feet from her. She skittishly jumped
back before remembering herself and holding out a hand
for a businesslike handshake.

'Well, Jacob. Thanks for dinner and…well, dinner. It
was really delicious.'

Jacob laughed softly before taking the proffered hand
and shaking it with a serious expression on his face. 'And
thank you for the presentation. It was enchanting.'

Holly looked at him blankly before he motioned to her
briefcase and she remembered what had really brought her
here in the first place.

'Of course. Well, I'm glad you like it. Come Monday
morning I will get on top of it and I'll contact…I'll get
Lydia to contact you later in the week with the final details.'

The lift binged and Holly let out a deep sigh of relief.

The doors opened and she stepped inside. Jacob leaned in slightly, his strong arms holding the lift doors open.

'In case you were wondering, I did tell my sister you were lovely, you know,' he admitted, looking her directly in the eye, his dimples out in full force.

Holly stared back, suddenly feeling very close to tears. He *really* had no idea. Jacob leaned in and kissed her lightly on the cheek, but the kiss lingered longer than was merely polite.

Holly sighed at his velvety touch and when he pulled away she saw that his eyes were closed tight. It took great restraint for her to stay put and when the doors began to close it took even greater strength to stop herself from wrenching them open and dragging him into the lift with her.

As the lift made its way downward Holly leant back onto the cool steel wall. The mirrored door in front of her revealed a very different expression from the one in the bathroom mirror half an hour before. Her lips were plump and now devoid of lipstick. Her eyes were bright and shining, wide and shell-shocked.

She found she could not draw her eyes away from the image until it finally wavered and split in two as the lift stopped on the bottom floor and the doors opened.

Jacob turned off the lights in the kitchen, leaving only those mood lights by his punching bag on. He had changed into track pants and running shoes and was strapping his wrists. But for the first time since he had installed the bag he didn't have the energy or the desire to hit it. He used to exercise himself into a frenzy to dissipate his frustrations. But tonight, with Holly's few well-chosen words, the aching feeling of injustice that had resided permanently in the pit of his stomach for so many years had eased.

He bounced around a bit, stretching out his shoulders and neck before throwing a few warm-up punches at the bag. All of a sudden the image of Holly standing there looking almost frightened as he'd slapped the bag flooded his mind.

He wondered why she hated boxing so much. Sure, a lot of women screwed up their dainty noses at the sport as they thought they were supposed to do, but he knew Holly was not false in that way. She really had something against it.

He had opened up and told her more of himself than he ever had to a mere 'friend of a friend', yet she had said not a word of her family or past. Was she simply a good listener or had she deliberately chosen not to reveal herself? Jacob found himself disappointed that she had not said anything. Or maybe he was disappointed that he had been so caught up in his own regrets that he had not thought to listen to her in the same way.

This would take some looking into. Not because he was interested in her in any personal way, of course, simply because he owed her. She had helped him more than she could know. And he wanted to return the favour.

Who was he kidding? He was interested. More and more so every time he met her. She was captivating. And truth be told he could hardly keep his hands off her. That scent: it reminded him of apples in summer. That hair: so thick and soft and ridiculously shiny.

But what was the use? No matter how attracted they were to each other, she was searching for something that he was unable to supply. But now, having had a taste of the delights Holly had on offer, he found he could not let it go at that. She was addictive. And he was hooked.

So what if she's on the hunt for a husband? Why can't I beg a little of her time until he comes along? I know we can have fun together until her Prince Charming appears.

But Jacob knew that as each day passed he found himself hoping her Prince Charming would not come along any time soon.

Holly angled her car onto the clear seaside street. No matter how hard she concentrated on the road ahead she could not shake one particular image from her mind: Jacob, self-professed risk-taker who was loath to put down roots, had in his top dresser drawer socks only, all neatly arranged by colour and fabric.

CHAPTER FIFTEEN

NINE o'clock Saturday morning Jacob could wait no longer. He picked up the phone and dialled.

'Beth, it's Jacob.'

'Jacob!' Beth said, her voice bright with pleasure. 'You've just missed Ben. He's gone down to the Dairy Bell to get me some Chocolate Nut-O Heaven ice cream.'

'A pregnancy craving, I take it.'

'I wish! I've always been a chockie-ice-cream addict. Did you want me to take a message?'

'I actually wanted to talk to you.'

'Okay. Talk away.'

'Well, it's about Holly—'

'Ooh, about time. Hang on a second while I get comfy.'

He listened as shuffling, scraping noises came through the other end of the phone.

'Well, you came to the right person,' Beth finally said. 'First thing you should know is that she prefers tulips to roses. She can't wear silver, she's allergic, so gold jewellery is the go—'

'Hold on, Beth. That's not what I was after. I'm not looking to propose, no matter how much you may have been planning and hoping. I'm just a little concerned about her.'

'Okay. What are you concerned about?'

'Well, she came over to my place last night—'

'Really? That's wonderful. She never told me—'

'Beth!'

'Yes?'

'Let me finish.'

'Okay, sorry. Buttoning lips right now.'

He smiled briefly as he had a feeling Beth had mimed buttoning her lips for real.

'She came over to my place last night to show me the proposal for Ana's party and she stayed for dinner.' Jacob paused, wondering how to explain what had happened next; he could barely deconstruct the order of events himself. 'Anyway, after dinner she saw the punching bag. You know the one I've always had in the corner of the lounge room? And she freaked out.'

'Freaked out how?' Beth asked, and Jacob was sure he heard real concern in his voice.

'Well, she chastised me for the boxing match at Fun and Games and for my Ali gloves. But the punching bag had her quaking. She seemed almost frightened.' Jacob decided he would have to spell it out. 'Why is Holly so against boxing?'

'Why shouldn't she be?' Beth asked, her voice excessively light. 'Many women are. I find it repulsive, grown men beating each other up. All that he-man, master-of-the-universe stuff. Most unattractive.'

'But it was more than that. I know it was. Was she…has she been hit before? Is that it?'

'No, Jacob. She was not hit.' But Beth's pause spoke volumes. He was onto something.

'Well, then, what is it? She's all messed up about something and it's driving me mad.'

'I think you should ask her that, Jacob.'

'I did, sort of.'

'Well, it's up to her to tell you.'

'So there is something to tell?' Jacob persevered.

'Jacob, I can't.'

Jacob swore under his breath. 'I was expecting you to

tell me…I don't know. Look I'm sorry. I shouldn't have come to you with this.'

'That's okay. Don't be sorry. Be careful.'

'I'll let you go. Say hi to Ben.'

'Sure.'

And then Jacob hung up.

Nine-thirty Saturday morning the phone rang. Holly ran out of the bathroom wrapped in a big fluffy towel. She ran on the tips of her toes so she would not leave wet footprints on the carpet, and grabbed the cordless phone from its cradle in the hallway.

'Hello?'

'Hello,' Jacob said, this time clearly not feeling the need to introduce himself. His voice low and ominous. And sexy and heart-wrenching.

'Hi.' Holly stood, dripping on the carpet, the phone clasped tightly to her ear as a heavy silence sizzled over the phone lines for a couple of uncomfortable moments.

'It's about Ana's party.'

'Of course.' She tried not to sound so disappointed. *What, were you expecting a proposal?*

'I'd like to change the location if possible.'

Holly frowned as her attention zoomed in on the party quick smart. She had spent a good deal of time picking out the perfect Lincoln Holdings-owned venue.

'All right. I had only pencilled us in at that banquet hall, so we can cancel no problem. Was there something in particular you did not like about my choice?'

'I would just like to hold it somewhere else.'

'Did you have this *somewhere else* in mind? Somewhere we can book with only a week's notice?'

'Actually I do. If I could pick you up at around noon I'll take you there for lunch.'

Lunch? Not likely. She had promised herself no more time alone with Jacob, if only for the sake of her own sanity. Beth often said, 'What goes up must come down', so shouldn't that be the same for love? If you could fall in love it should be just as easy to fall out of love, so that was what she was going to do.

She cradled the phone between her chin and her shoulder, grabbing her towel with one hand as she scrambled for a pen and paper with the other.

'There's no need for you to take me, really. Just let me know the name of the place and I'll look after it on Monday. During work hours.' *There, that should put him in his place.*

'Wouldn't it be better to have it settled straight away? Considering we do only have a week's notice, as you said?'

Holly gritted her teeth to stop herself from saying that was his fault, not hers. 'Okay. But how about I meet you there?' Besides, being in a restaurant they would not exactly be alone; maybe she *could* stretch the boundaries of her promise. 'Just give me the address—'

'Much easier if I pick you up. I'll see you at twelve.'

And then Jacob hung up. Holly looked at the phone for a moment before slamming it back down on the cradle. She picked it up and slammed it again for good measure.

'You are so infuriating!' she shouted to the empty hallway as she padded back into the bathroom.

At a couple of minutes before midday Holly's doorbell rang. She grabbed her bag, quickly checked her make-up in the hall mirror.

Feeling more nervous than before any of her blind dates, she ran a hand down either side of her baby-blue knee-length dress, fixed the collar on the matching cropped jacket, and checked her stockings had no runs. That morning every little choice had taken on new significance. Her dress, her lipstick, the way she wore her hair—she wanted to be as attractive for him as she could possibly be.

She pointed an accusing finger at her reflection. 'You have no will-power.'

Her breath caught in her throat at the sight that met her when she opened the door. Jacob stood before her in jeans, a bulky cream sweater and a soft brown leather bomber jacket. Even dressed down he was stunning. Her heart leapt in her chest and she knew, no matter how many times during the long sleepless night before she had told herself she was overestimating her feelings for him, she was wrong.

She loved him.

Holly soon saw that he was giving her the same once-over but she knew that, sadly, his thoughts were less altruistic than her own.

'You didn't have to get all dressed up for me,' Jacob joked as he took the house key out of Holly's hand and locked the front door for her. He led her down the footpath.

'These are work clothes,' Holly said stiffly as her judgment came back to her. 'And this is a work meeting.'

'Yes, ma'am.' Jacob saluted. 'I didn't mean to intimate that I was in any way displeased. On the contrary, you look absolutely beautiful.'

He looked her over again, his eyes full of the praise he had willingly stated. Holly felt her self-restraint dissolving under his gaze.

Jacob opened the passenger door to his car and waited until she was settled before he jogged around to the driver's side. He gunned the engine and pulled out onto the road.

Holly waited for the other shoe to drop. She waited for

the cross-examination or the apology or something, anything to be said about their surprising dinner the night
before. But he sat back, whistling along with the jazz sta-
tion on the car stereo.

'So,' Holly said, breaking the silence, 'where are you
taking me?'

'Ah, now that would be telling.' Jacob tapped the side
of his nose.

Holly laughed, dumbfounded by his playful mood. 'And
what is wrong with telling?'

Jacob pointed at the car stereo. 'Don't you love this
song? This version was recorded in nineteen sixty-eight in
this little pub on Bourbon St—'

'Jacob!'

'You talk too much, woman. Life is too short for so
many questions. I order you to sit back, relax, and enjoy
the ride.'

Holly gave in. 'Fine.' She sat back against the lambs-
wool seat covers, snug in the heated car listening to the
soft jazz playing on the stereo. She turned her head to the
side and watched Melbourne go by through the tinted windows.

Jacob glanced towards Holly several times, wishing he
could decipher the thoughts behind her calm, cool gaze.
He itched to launch straight into a direct Q and A about
Holly's past that Beth had all but admitted was brutal.

But he also had the feeling she would more likely open
the door and jump from a moving car than be forced to
talk about it. He bit his tongue and drove. There would be
time for questions later.

After fifteen minutes of companionable silence, Jacob
pulled into a familiar driveway.

'This is Lunar.'

'It certainly is.' He chose one of the free staff car parks, pulled on the handbrake, shot out of the car and around to Holly's door before she had even unbuckled her belt.

'*This* is your suggestion for a new location for Anabella's party?'

'Why? You don't think it would be perfect?' Jacob took her by the hand and pulled her from her seat.

'Of course. I love this place and it's much more appropriate for what I originally had in mind. I have a good relationship with the owners so we may have some luck booking it on short notice.'

'I've already checked and it's fine.'

Holly was a little put out that he had gone over her head, especially after his constant avowals that he wanted to stay out of the loop. 'Okay. But when did you speak to the owners? Between last night and now? You could have told me earlier if you weren't happy—'

'I am the owner, Holly.'

'You? No, you're not. Herman and Gina have owned the place for ever.'

Jacob placed light hands on the tops of her arms as though he knew she would fall over without his support. 'Not anymore.'

He let her go, slipping his hands in his trouser pockets, and Holly felt bereft, cool where her arms had been lit by his warmth only moments before.

'The deal came through midnight last night. Sorry I couldn't say anything. Confidentiality clauses and all that. Besides, after meeting you here for lunch that day I had an odd feeling that you would pick Lunar for the party even without my advice.' He shrugged. 'No matter. It's all worked out okay in the end.'

Holly felt devastated, as if she had let him down. As if

choosing Lunar would have been a sign and she had failed. She felt like running after him and tugging on his arm and begging him to believe it had been her first choice. Beth would have been tickled to see her reaching for signs in that way.

'Are you okay with it being here?' he asked.

'Of course. I adore this place. This has been my lucky place ever since I started out at Cloud Nine. I bring all of my new clientele here.'

And then something he had said another time came back to her.

'You're not going to refurbish, are you? You're not going to change Lunar and then sell it off, like you did with your apartment block?'

Jacob's eyes narrowed. 'You don't think that if you took clients somewhere else they would not sign with you, do you?'

'No,' Holly answered, though not sure if that was the whole truth.

'Because it is you they love, not the meeting venue.'

Her heart tumbled. There was one particular client she would do anything to have love her.

'Or the magic briefcase or the lucky suit.'

Holly noted mentally that she would have to kill Lydia. 'You didn't answer my question.'

'I've owned the place for about twelve hours—how can I answer that?'

'If you've been after it for ages then I am certain you know exactly what you plan to do with it.'

'Perhaps,' he answered under his breath.

A waiter led them over to Holly's usual table.

'Well, since we know Lunar is available and you know I approve we really don't need to stay, do we?'

'We are here now. It's lunchtime. We may as well eat.'

She sat back, fuming, crossed her arms and refused to look at the menu. After a few moments of uncomfortable silence, she found Jacob watching her intently.

'What? Do I have something on my face?'

'That scar.' He pointed to a small straight scar at the top of the ridge of her nose. 'How did you get that?'

Holly's hand flew to the spot; she knew exactly the scar he meant. She flicked her head in a practised move so that a lock of fringe hair fell to cover the exact spot. Still seething, she looked back up and with a false smile answered, 'It's nothing. Just a silly accident as a kid, that's all.'

'What sort of accident?' Jacob persisted.

'It really doesn't matter. It's not an interesting story, I promise.'

'Tell me anyway.'

'I'd rather not.' Holly knew her voice was rising but she could not help it.

'Come on. Holly, I know you are hiding something big. Something you would rather I don't know.'

Am I so transparent? she thought, close to laughing hysterically. He was being so gentle, so reassuring. But how would he be if she said, *Fine, Jacob. I have been hiding something. I seem to have fallen in love with you.*

'I told you about my family,' he said, 'about my childhood. I want you to know that you can share the same with me.'

Where had the teasing grin gone? That had been much easier to resist than the offer of solace and compassion from the man who had stolen her heart.

Holly swallowed hard as her ears began to ring and the stories and memories welled up inside her. After years of learning to calm her nerves and the swelling tide that once overcame her, she suddenly felt a great desire to confide in this man.

She wanted him to know her inside and out. She felt that she would be cheating him if she did not share with him what he had shared with her. And she knew in her heart that he would not judge her. She uncrossed her arms, her hands slipping to take a hold of the napkin on her lap in a firm grip.

'You really want to know how I got this scar?' she asked quietly, needing a final push.

Jacob was shocked that she had demurred so soon. He sat forward, clasped his hands on the table, and looked deep into her troubled eyes.

'Yes, Holly. I really want to know.'

She began in a quiet voice. 'It was at the Hidden Valley Greyhound Course, of all places.'

Of course, Jacob thought, *the colonel mentioned it at the fundraiser.*

'I was there with my dad. He had gone missing, which wasn't unusual. For hours, which wasn't unusual. After a while, once I was hungry, I went looking for him. I was a kid but the guys there knew me well and I could go where I pleased. I headed to the bar, scampering between the tall tree-trunk legs of the regulars when one guy stopped me. Picked me up in his arms, his eyes bloodshot from drink, and he asked me what the hell I was doing there. He could barely hold himself up, much less me. And he dropped me. I landed badly, my face hit a bar stool and I was knocked out. I came to in the hospital.'

'Your father must have been beside himself.'

'Well, he certainly was not beside me. The colonel was there and he had taken charge. Carried me to the course ambulance and forced his way into that van with me to ride to the hospital. He stayed with me through the day and took me home to stay with him and his wife that night. And the next and the next.'

'Your dad?'

'He showed up about three days later. Turned up at the door with a big grin and a pocket full of cash and took me home.'

'Where had he been?'

She shrugged. 'Who knows. Back at the track, maybe? Or perhaps he had found a soul mate, another guy onto a good thing, a sure bet, a quick fix. Or maybe he had been in on a fixed boxing match and was just holed up in whichever motel we were currently living in, watching the fight on pay TV. Any of the above would have been a typical day in the life.'

'Was the man in the bar charged with assault?'

'Gosh, no. The racecourse could have gone under from something like that. Then where would my dad have been without a place to leave the kid on the weekends?'

He had never heard her bitter before. She was masking it with humour but the sadness shone through all the same.

'It was okay, really. Though the colonel has never forgiven himself for not reporting the incident.' Holly shook her head in genuine amazement. 'He saved me that day. Showed me what regular life could be, with rules and boundaries and a place to call home. I help him out every year now, help keep his dear racecourse afloat. I owe him that much if not everything.'

Jacob wanted to leap around the table, take her in his arms, and promise that nobody would hurt her ever again.

The waiter arrived with their drinks and Jacob took the quiet moment to absorb the story of Holly's upbringing and to try to reconcile it with the woman sitting before him.

She was so refined, so elegant, she knew where to eat, how to dress, and organised A-list functions for the city's rich and famous. You would think she had grown up with money, with prestige, with a chauffeur and a grand home.

But she had created herself from nothing. The educated accent, the prestigious job, the VIP contacts, she had cultivated them from the ground up.

Yet underneath that perfect façade was a real fear of change, of being abandoned, being out of control. It explained her desire to contain the passionate and impulsive side to her personality. No matter how she waved away her father's lax responsibility, she was frightened that she had inherited his hot-blooded nature so she was constantly trying to be more calm, more patient and more composed.

As the waiter left Holly's mobile phone rang. She scrambled to answer it quick smart, as though it were a lifeline.

'Hello, Holly Denison speaking.'

Jacob sipped on his drink, watching Holly carefully as he listened openly to the one-sided conversation.

'Right, I see. No, I wasn't busy,' Holly said, deliberately not looking at him. 'I'll be right there.' She hung up her phone.

She pushed back her chair and stood. 'Jacob. I'm sorry. I won't be able to stay for lunch. One of my clients has a Women in Film luncheon on Monday and it seems the guest of honour is trying to pull out.'

'But it's your day off. Can't one of the others look after it?'

'Ordinarily yes. But this client is quite temperamental and will only deal with me. She won't even take Lydia's phone calls. I'm sorry.'

Jacob went to stand as well but Holly all but pushed him back into his seat.

'No, you stay. I'll catch a cab. I'll talk to you later in the week. Bye.'

Jacob could do nothing but watch her go.

CHAPTER SIXTEEN

LATE Saturday night Jacob rang the doorbell. He rubbed his hands together to relieve them of the freezing cold, and shuffled from foot to foot so his toes would not go numb. It took several moments for Ben and Beth to answer the door together.

'Jacob!' Ben said. 'It's almost midnight. What are you doing here?'

'You look terrible. Are you okay?' Beth added as she stepped around Ben to take a closer look.

'She told me.'

'Who told you what?' Ben asked. His hair was flattened on one side and Jacob worried he had caught them asleep.

But Jacob saw the understanding dawn on Beth's face. She took her husband by the arm, pulled him out of the way and motioned for him to go get tea, then guided Jacob inside and onto the couch.

'Holly. She told me about her dad at the racecourse. And the scar. And the colonel. And…that's all.'

Beth nodded and looked over his bedraggled appearance. 'Have you been drinking?'

'No. Though I wanted to. I have been sitting in a bar not far from here for the last several hours. Thinking and eating stale beer nuts.'

'And what were you thinking about?'

'I was thinking about finding the guy who gave her that scar and breaking his nose.' His fists clenched in his lap. 'Or finding her father and giving him a piece of my mind.'

'Not much chance of that. Holly's father died several years ago.'

'Good,' he whispered under his breath and was amazed at the vehemence in his own voice. It was rare for him to become so impassioned. Not over business ideas. Not even over Anabella. He'd thought he had long since learnt not to care so much. But in that moment he felt so worked up, he could hardly think straight.

Beth took him by the hand, drawing his lapsing attention to her face.

'I told you the truth when I said he never hit Holly, but his apathy damaged her in other ways.'

Jacob listened intently, latching onto Beth's every word as though they were the salvation that could drag him out of this unnerving mood.

'Her dad was a drifter,' she continued. 'He dabbled in amateur boxing but was never good enough to make a living, but unfortunately learnt enough to use his skills to settle disagreements when the need arose. He never held down a proper job for long. He usually lost them after turning up with a black eye from a pub brawl the night before or by just not turning up at all. I'm pretty sure Holly even saw her dad in a few of his later fights. All losses, from what I know. So Holly has understandably never been so hot for the combat sports.'

'Did you ever meet him?' Jacob asked.

'Holly's father? Yes, I did.'

Jacob stared at her, willing her to go on.

'I stayed with them during the holidays, first year uni. He was living in a caravan then. Had been for a year or so. The longest they had stayed in one place, I think. I liked him. He took us to the ballet and to this bizarre underground modern art gallery. He had more energy in his little finger than anyone I had ever met. I thought Holly was so lucky to have such a cool father.'

'But, he left her for dead in a bar.' Jacob felt his face growing red with anger. 'And from what I gathered him leaving her to her own devices for days at a time was not unusual. I would hardly call that lucky.'

'I know that now but at the time that wanderlust and lack of responsibility was tantalizing. For a college kid, still living at home, it seemed close to heaven. Little did I know Holly would have given away all her freedom to be able to live in a normal home like I did.'

Jacob bit his bottom lip raw. It hit him that Beth had just described his own life for the past ten years. Wanderlust, lack of responsibility, freedom. They seemed like such hollow pursuits when on the outside looking in.

Ben came in at that moment with a tray of coffee and biscuits. He poured some out for himself and Jacob, along with a herbal tea for his pregnant wife. She sent him a loving smile before continuing.

'It wasn't until after his funeral, when Holly and I stayed up all through the night and she told me the story of the scar amongst others. If he ever felt the need to travel or disappear the fact that he had a child in his care did not stop him. Sometimes when he did his disappearing acts he took Holly with him so that she would miss weeks of school at a time. Sometimes he would leave her in a motel with some cash and the manager's phone number in case of emergency.'

He pictured Holly, as a little girl, with long brunette hair flying behind her as she ran about the racecourse and he felt sick. 'She must have so much pent-up rage against the man for what he did to her.'

'I don't know about that. You would have had to see them together. It was amazing. They either adored each other or hated each other from one day to the next. He doted on her; she was his little angel, yet he left her. It has made her the resilient, ingenious, forgiving woman she is today.'

He knew she was right. Holly had said pretty much the same thing to him before, that it was the highs *and* the lows that created a well-rounded personality. But it still did not stop him feeling so much anger towards any man who could cause her that sort of pain. He leant his head in his hands, rubbing furiously at his red eyes. 'God. What a mess.'

Jacob finally came up for air and saw Beth smiling at him. How could she be smiling at such a moment?

'What?'

'You're the mess, Jacob. Holly's fine. She has her moments but deep down she is fine. She's taken from it what she can and grown up.'

'Then why did she say she is scared of me? Why does she run every time it looks like we may have a proper conversation?'

When neither of his hosts made to answer Jacob deflated, all but running out of fight. 'I just had to know what made her tick, didn't I? So, I sat there and dared her to tell me about the scar on her nose. I was such a bully. And that's the last thing she needs.'

Beth smiled. 'Don't worry about it, Jacob. Poor Ben knew none of this when he took her to that stupid boxing match of yours the other week. But he also knows she is big enough and old enough to look after herself. That night she made the adult decision to walk away, to simply not be a part of the crowd, and everything turned out just fine.'

But that was Jacob's main worry. What if because of a myriad unfortunate coincidences, she made the decision not to be a part of his life. The thought of her pulling away so far he would never see her again made something ache deep inside him. But before he had the chance to really think about what that ache could be Ben spoke up.

'What do you want from her, Jacob?'

'What do you mean?' Jacob asked, surprised by Ben's suddenly protective tone.

'I mean that you all but told me that you had no interest in Holly, yet all I can see is you actively pursuing her, creating this last-minute party for Ana. And now you sound like you are about to fall to pieces because she may be shying away from you. What do you want from her?'

'I don't know.' That much was true. He wanted his comfortable, impenetrable old life, and at the same time he wanted her. But he knew he couldn't have both.

Which was the bigger sacrifice? Giving up the seamless wall he had spent a good decade building around himself? Giving up the secure knowledge that nobody could touch him, hurt him, want more from him than he could ever provide?

Or giving up her? Giving up the chance to have her blossom in his arms? Giving up the conviction and hope and delight that he drew from her without diminishing any of her own conviction and hope and delight?

For the first time, in a really long time, he felt the choice was there for the taking.

'Well, maybe it's about time you should know,' Ben said, 'because if you don't want to pursue Holly seriously, you really ought to leave her be. And if you really do feel something for her, and want to know her and help her, you really should be talking to her about this and not to us. Now, it's almost midnight and Beth really doesn't need this sort of excitement right now, so I want you to go home and sleep this off and decide what you want. We'll support you either way, but only once you're sure.'

And then Ben stood up, bringing a shocked Beth to her feet with him.

Jacob rose too. 'I am sorry to have come at such a time. I should go home.'

He kissed Beth on the cheek and then patted Ben on the arm. 'I'll see you.'

'Monday at work,' Ben added, his expression uncompromising.

'Monday at work,' Jacob promised.

Monday, Beth and Holly met for an early morning yoga class.

'Have you spoken to Jacob recently?' Beth asked.

'No, not so recently.'

'Since the weekend?'

'Umm, no, not since the weekend.'

'When are you planning to speak to him again?'

'What is with all these questions, Beth? The party is in five days so I will most likely speak to Jacob before then. Does that satisfy you?'

'Sure. But does that satisfy you?'

'Excuse me?' Holly asked loud enough for the yoga instructor to look over at them with narrowed eyes. Holly smiled in apology before turning back to her friend. 'What do you mean by that?'

'Why don't you two just stop dancing around each other and go for it?' Beth asked in exasperation.

'Go for what?'

'Date him or kiss him or something. Forget about your grand theory. And forget about marrying him or anyone else for now.' Beth rolled her eyes in exasperation. 'You know how when you decide to buy a new pair of shoes, you can never find ones you really like. But as soon as

you go looking for a new dress, you find the perfect shoes
instead?'

Holly stopped stretching long enough to stare blankly at
her friend.

'Just take each other for a test drive is all I'm saying.
No expectations. No strings. Just become involved.'

No strings, Holly thought. *If only.* A week before she
had scoffed at the suggestion but now she wished it were
only possible. She wished she could confide in her friend
that all of her wishes were coming true one on top of the
other and she had no idea if they were really what she
wanted in the first place.

She had found the perfect man, and had fallen in love.
Wish number one come true.

She was on the verge of landing the job of a lifetime.
Wish number two come true.

But they came with a catch. They were all wrapped up
in the unknowable whims of one person. A person she
knew was as attracted to her as she was to him. A person
who had made her tempting offers but no promises. A
person who had proven that when trouble arose, he flew
the coop.

There was simply no way Holly could place her whole
future happiness in the arms of Jacob Lincoln.

So what to do?

Pursue an affair and forget the job?

Take the job and hope her feelings would fade over
time?

Or maybe it would be best to leave both prospects well
enough alone and start afresh. She had been perfectly
happy before bumping into him that day on the street.
Maybe not perfectly happy but at least she did not feel as
if she were being torn in a million different directions.

Couldn't she go back to the way it was before she had

met him? Working day and night on myriad one-off projects? Dating every now and then when she had the time and the inclination?

If only.

She told Beth all she was comfortable revealing right then.

'We have kissed, actually.'

'What? When? What was it like? Why didn't you tell me?'

'Once outside your place and then at his apartment. It was lovely. And I didn't tell you because I don't know what to make of it all.'

'Did he kiss you or did you kiss him?'

'He kissed me. Both times.'

Beth threw her hands up in exasperation.

'Holly! What are you waiting for? He obviously likes you. I mean, he's spoken of nothing else since our little dinner party.'

'Really?' Holly asked, unable to contain the intense pleasure she took from that one tiny validation. She so longed to confide in her friend but once she said out loud how she felt, that would only make it harder for it all to go away.

'Really. He came around to our place all worked up about a conversation you'd had at Lunar.'

'Oh. That.'

'Yes, that. You told him about your dad, I take it.'

'Mmm.'

'I think he's pretty worried that you see him primarily as a man without roots and with your history that would make you understandably wary.'

Holly kept quiet. Wary of what? Her mind reeled with the possibilities but she forced herself to rein them in.

'Jacob is a free spirit, like your dad, he has a strong

personality, like your dad, and happens to enjoy boxing, like your dad. This does not mean that he would ever leave you alone for weeks at a time without telling you where he is or where he's been.'

'I know he wouldn't.'

'I know you know.' Beth took her gently by the shoulders and made sure Holly looked her straight in the eye. 'Then why are you using it as an excuse not to go for broke with him?'

Holly struggled to free herself from Beth's strong grip, not wanting her friend to see the truth was hitting home. But she failed.

'Because Jacob is a good man and I think he really cares for you, and if you can't bring yourself to trust a man as good and kind and eligible as him then I don't see that there can be any hope that you will be able to find anyone you can trust.'

Holly looked up at Beth, tears welling in her eyes. 'I have never pretended to *like* Jacob. In fact, I have made it clear to you and he alike that he is not my type. Sure, we may have kissed and I may be…attracted to him, but that's all.'

That is so not all. But by God that will be all by the time I have worked him out of my system.

'I think my trusting him or not is irrelevant. Thanks for the advice, but it's really not necessary at this time.'

Holly gently pulled away from Beth, walked through the class to collect her towel, and left the room.

Friday night Holly relaxed by her roaring fire. She had just that day handed over the moment-to-moment management of Ana's party to Lydia. Lydia had all but knocked Holly off her feet as she'd lunged at her and enveloped her in a massive clinch of thanks. Holly had no doubt Lydia could handle any last-minute changes and she also knew there was no way she would be in the right frame of mind to look after them herself. She still had not decided if she would even turn up at all.

The phone rang at Holly's side.

'What time should I pick you up for the party?' Jacob asked not finding the need for even a 'hello' this time.

Holly sat bolt upright wondering if her thoughts had carried across the miles and reached him. She hadn't spoken to him in days, managing to avoid his phone calls and ignore his messages. But hearing his voice glide down the phone line, she was promptly sucked back into the same weak, deep, heartbreaking sensation she had tried all week to put behind her.

'You can't pick me up, Jacob.'

'Why not? I have a car. I have a driver's licence. There's nothing stopping me. And don't tell me you're not coming because it would simply kill Ana and I know you don't have it in you to do that.'

At least the question of her not going had been decided for her.

But despite his flippant tone, she could tell he felt as strained as she did. And she knew without a doubt it was because he was feeling sorry for her. It always happened that way. Once anybody found out about her childhood, they changed around her. They patted her on the arm and smiled softly, as though any sudden movement would set her off. And she could not stand the thought of looking at Jacob through her own eyes filled with love, only to have him looking back at her in pity.

'I too have a car and do not need a lift as I am perfectly capable of driving myself to the party in said car.'

'Fine. Then you can come and pick me up.'

'No! Besides, I have to get there early and—'

'No, you don't. I already know you've handed over control to Lydia for the day. She told me. You will be a guest just like any other.'

Once again, Holly silently cursed Lydia for her big mouth.

'I just think it would be best if we make our separate ways to Lunar tomorrow.'

'But *I* think we should go together. A real date this time, not just us bumping into each other or working together.'

'If Beth has been match-making just forget about it. Please don't think I asked her to—'

'Holly.' His voice sounded nervous and it stopped her short. '*I'm* asking you if you would like to come to the party with me as my date. Not through Beth. Not through Ben. *I* would like to spend the evening at your side.'

Unbidden tears welled in Holly's eyes and ran down her quivering cheeks.

'I don't think that's such a good idea,' she whispered.

'Why not? Do you already have a date?' Jacob asked, his tone joking.

'Yes, I do,' Holly lied before she knew what she was doing.

'You do?' he asked, obviously shocked. 'Hell. Holly, don't tell me you are back on the husband hunt again!'

It was time to put her personal affiliation with Jacob to rest. Once and for all. It was the only way she could have the peace and quiet and time to heal her heart and he would not feel the need to see her out of pity. And what better way than to use his own presumption?

'I was never off the hunt. Just took a hiatus until I got some…work out of the way. Now we're back into the swing. Me and Ben.'

'You can't be serious.'

'Well, I am.' She felt her voice becoming slightly hysterical. 'Anyway, Ben and Beth are picking me...and my date...up. It's simpler for me to go with Ben and Beth. It's just simpler.'

'So, you'd rather go with Ben.'

'And Beth,' she repeated.

'Why did you choose Ben to look for a husband for you?' His voice was low and flat, the earlier emotion now completely sapped away.

'Well, I love Ben, and I knew that he would only set me up with someone he thought would be nice to me.'

'Are you sure that it isn't simply because, as you said, you love Ben?'

Holly's eyes grew wide in shock; she clutched the phone hard and pressed it tight to her ear.

'Jacob! You can't think that of me. That is a terrible thing to say. I mean, Beth is my very best friend in the whole world.'

'We can't choose who we love Holly.' His voice sounded subdued and wounded. It took all of her self-control not to unreservedly agree with his sentiments and tell him who had really stolen her heart.

'Even so, I am not in love with Ben. Ben is lovely and he puts up with me, which is a big plus in his favour, but I've never, ever seen him as anything more than a big brother.'

After a long pause during which Holly felt her heart beat faster, Jacob whispered, 'Come with me, Holly.'

'I can't,' Holly choked out, her emotions rising in her throat.

'Fine, then. I'll see you there. And if there is no mystery date on your arm I will know why, no matter how you try to justify your actions.'

And with that, Jacob hung up.

Holly stared at the phone in her hand for a number of

seconds before she placed it in its cradle. She thought hard and fast before picking up the phone and dialling.

'Hi, Beth,' Holly said.

'Holly? How you feeling?'

'Fine. I'm fine. Sorry for the yelling and—'

'Oh, shut up,' Beth said, laughing. 'What can I do for you?'

'I need you guys to find me a date.'

'Not that again. I made a promise to Ben that we would never spring anything like that on him ever again. Ever. Or at least this week anyway.'

'Look, I don't want a life partner this time. Just someone who isn't busy tomorrow night.'

'But you are busy tomorrow night, with Anabella's party.'

'That's the point. I need a date for the party.'

'Well, not trying to sound like a broken record but…if I'm not mistaken Jacob was going to ask a certain young lady we both know and love so your problem may be solved.'

'But that is the problem. I don't want to go with Jacob, so I told him that I already had a date, so now I have to take someone else with me so he will stop bugging me. How about Derek from Payroll?'

Beth paused meaningfully. 'Okay, let me get this straight. You are asking me to set you up with Derek the weed so that the gorgeous, charismatic and highly eligible Jacob Lincoln will stop bugging you?'

'That's right. Derek seems harmless enough and I need harmless right now.'

'Now you are really worrying me. It's one thing deciding to get married without even having a boyfriend, but wanting a date with Derek the weed over Jacob the hunk is a whole different kind of madness.'

'Beth, you don't think I have a crush on Ben, do you?' Holly said, unable to hold it in any longer.

'Whoa. I certainly didn't see that one coming.'

'Well, do you?'

'No, I don't.'

'Jacob thinks I'm in love with Ben.'

Beth laughed sweetly on the other end of the phone and Holly could have strangled her. She felt so rotten she was sick to the stomach and all Beth could do was giggle.

'Jacob does not think you have a crush on Ben, honey. Jacob is having a hard time figuring you out, that's all. And I think it's hard for him that you are not falling into his arms as readily as he is used to, or as readily as he is falling into yours.'

Holly's head swam.

'Now, as for Ben, I know he represents safety and contentment to you and that's what you think you want. But what you actually want is someone who loves you.'

'So, Jacob is wrong?'

'About this, yes. But about knowing that he should be the one at your side at the party, no. About that I believe he is very right.'

'Beth,' Holly pleaded. 'I can't. Please call Derek for me.'

'Okay,' Beth sighed. 'I'll call the weed. But only because I gain so much enjoyment from your lunacy.'

'Thank you.' Holly breathed a sigh of relief. 'I'll talk to you later.'

'Bye, sweetie.'

And they both hung up.

CHAPTER SEVENTEEN

SATURDAY night Derek was unable to pick Holly up as he did not own a car. He had offered to meet her at the bus stop since they were on the same route but Ben and Beth kindly intervened and offered to pick them up at their respective homes.

Lydia was already waiting outside Lunar when they arrived and in her simple, elegant suit, slicked-back hair and glasses perched on the end of her nose, she was a revelation.

'All's well, Holly,' Lydia whispered, her buoyant effervescence seeping through the conservative exterior. 'I've never seen any event go so smoothly. The chefs are smiling, the bar is well stocked, and the guests of honour are relaxed. It's a miracle.'

'Enjoy it, Lydia. You're doing great.'

Holly was instantly on the lookout for Jacob, telling herself she wanted him in her sights so that she could avoid him. But there was no avoiding the willowy young woman who swooped upon her as soon as she entered the main room.

'You just have to be Holly!' the woman exclaimed.

Holly then noticed the crooked front teeth and dimpled cheeks. 'And you must be Anabella. You look so much like your brother.'

'I know, though hopefully I'm at least a little *prettier*. Now let me have a good look at you.'

Anabella held Holly at arm's length and looked her over

like an old aunt who had not seen her niece since she was
a little girl.

'I believe the word Jacob used was "gorgeous",'
Anabella said. She turned to Beth and Ben, her eyes twinkling indulgently. 'And from what I hear, you two introduced my darling brother to this one.'

'Not quite,' Beth said, 'though we have helped them
along as much as possible, I cannot claim ownership of
orchestrating their first meeting. It was purely accidental.
Kismet, I say, though some people beg to differ.'

'I heard. Bumped into each other in the street and he
had to help her pick up her belongings. I couldn't stop
laughing when he told me. My big burly brother helping
a damsel in distress. Priceless!'

Holly could sense Beth glaring at her open-mouthed;
shock, confusion, an inkling and then complete understanding playing across her face. Holly shook her head,
no, but she knew that would not be the end of it.

'This sensational hunk of a man is my fiancé, Michael.'
Ana pulled a stranger forward. He was slightly shorter than
she was, several years older with a neat, greying beard and
greying hair at his temples. He was as soft as Ana was
striking and his eyes rarely left Ana's face. 'Mikey, this is
Ben, Jake's right-hand man, and Ben's wife, Beth, and
inside her big tummy is their first.'

Holly felt an ache deep down inside her as she stood
there surrounded by such an abundance of love. Her eyes
reluctantly roved over the crowd looking for a certain familiar face.

'And this gorgeous creature,' Ana said, looking to
Holly, who snapped back to attention at the sound of her
nickname, 'is the woman who has sent Jacob into such a
mope the last few days. I really can't forgive you for that,

Holly. Whatever you did it has made him a nuisance to live with.'

'Who is a nuisance?' Derek had returned from depositing the ladies' coats in the cloakroom.

'Derek,' Beth said, her eyes bright with laughter, 'this is Ana and Michael, our gracious hosts. Ana, Michael, this is Derek Gordon. He works in Payroll with Lincoln Holdings.'

'I'm here with Holly,' he clarified to the group in general.

Holly saw Ana shoot a questioning look to Beth whose furrowed brow and shaking head were enough to explain the situation. That was all Holly needed, for word to get back to Jacob that Derek was superfluous.

'Well, it is nice to meet you, Derek,' Ana said.

'Likewise, I'm sure,' he answered, looking anywhere but at his hosts. 'Holly, it's time we circulate.'

He took Holly by the elbow and dragged her away. They reached the bar in record time and Holly ordered a glass of champagne.

'No, Holly,' Derek insisted as he pulled the glass from her hand and handed it back to the astonished bartender. 'You don't need a simulated high tonight. You just leave that up to me.'

He ordered two matching cranberry juices. 'Good for the kidneys.'

Holly defiantly pushed the juice aside, grabbed her original flute of bubbly and took a great big swig. As she spun around, aiming to get as far away from her appalling date as soon as possible, she stepped smack bang into an unmovable object. It was Jacob.

'Oh, hello, Jacob,' she said breathily. Though his beautiful hazel eyes glowered down at her, her heart danced a rumba at his presence.

'Where is Ben?' he asked.

Holly came back down to earth with a thud.

'He is with Beth, I expect.' Holly made sure her tone was light in front of Derek, who she knew was hanging on every word.

'Really? I would have thought you would not have let him out of your sight.'

'Yes, well, you thought wrong. Beth and Ben were chatting away with *another* happy couple when I last saw them.' She maintained a warning glint in her eye. 'We met Anabella and Michael at the front door.'

Jacob's eyes narrowed slightly as Derek moved in close behind Holly and wrapped an arm about her waist.

'I know you, don't I?' Jacob asked, sounding terribly imperious as he stared down his nose at the offending arm.

'Sure do, Mr Lincoln. I work for you. Derek Gordon. Payroll.'

'He's with you?' Jacob asked Holly, his tone incredulous, ignoring Derek's outstretched hand.

'Surely am, dear fellow. All it took was six months of badgering before she finally acquiesced. Helpful hint. Persistence, dear boy, will never let you down.'

Holly took a quick sip of champagne, willing herself not to thrust away Derek's wandering hands.

'How are you enjoying the party?' Holly asked, trying to deflect Jacob's attention away from her crumbling charade. 'Is it everything you thought it would be?'

It was perfect and Holly knew it. There was not a thing he could possibly fault. But he merely shrugged and shot a meaningful glance at Derek.

'Don't draft the press release just yet.'

She all but coughed on her champagne bubbles. Was that another hint that she would have to choose between a man and the job? He was playing with fire if that was the case. That was one too many times he had changed the rules to suit himself and she'd had enough.

'Oh, don't worry about that, Jacob,' she said through clenched teeth. 'Knowing full well your aversion towards obligations, I wouldn't dream of banking on a guarantee from you.'

Jacob flinched and she knew every word had hit its mark. He paled and a pair of misshapen red blotches stained his smooth cheeks. He looked as though she had slapped him square across the face.

But she kept her eyes locked onto his, determined not to budge, not to back down, not to be moved by his wretched expression. If she had set out to make him hate her, she might have succeeded.

Jacob finally dragged his tortured eyes from her and seemed to notice Derek anew, his expression hardening until it closed to her completely.

'I guess when Holly began this husband hunt of hers she opened her eyes to previously unexplored avenues of experience.'

'What's this?' Derek asked.

Holly was instantly red-faced. *Touché.*

'I guess she has made her choice. Well, I will leave you two lovebirds to it. I've never seen Holly look more lovely or happier than she is tonight and I guess she owes it all to you. Looks like the best man won here, Derek.'

Jacob nodded gravely and walked away.

'If what he said was true,' Derek said, 'though you seem a right corker of a girl, I promise I won't be proposing to you before the night is out. I hope that doesn't put a damper on your evening.'

Holly was finally able to drag her eyes from Jacob's retreating back. 'Not at all, Derek, I promise you with all my heart.'

'Good, good. Never actually met him before, you know. Seen him in the halls and that. Seems a decent enough fellow.'

'Yes, he is decent enough,' Holly agreed as her eyes were once again drawn to him. The most decent man she had ever met; a man with a good heart, a remarkable mind, and no false airs. And she had just cruelly thrown his deepest regrets back in his face, all to cover up her own feeble fears.

She watched Jacob circulate through the crowd. Ana came bounding up to him and enveloped him in a bear-hug. Over her shoulder Jacob said something to Michael, which sent the reserved man into uproarious laughter. Ana pulled away and hit Jacob playfully on the shoulder and he winced in mock pain. Holly could see even from that distance the love and respect Jacob brought out in people just as he had so easily brought it out in her.

And now she had done her best to make him hate her. Oh, what had she done?

'Well, come on, then,' Derek said. 'We had better find our table. Don't want to get there and find someone has switched our place cards.'

The dinner felt painfully slow as Holly counted every passing second until it would be polite to leave. The highlight of the dinner was when she danced with Derek; he motioned to the staircase, which led to several well-appointed rooms above the restaurant. 'The stairway to heaven,' he called it. And he was deadly serious.

Despite herself, she cracked up laughing. And at that moment caught Jacob watching her. For a split second, she felt his fuming gaze from across the room. Then he blinked, the cold façade once more on show, and her heart sank even lower.

After the speeches, Holly excused herself and went to the bathroom. And Beth followed.

'The man, on the street,' Beth began without preamble, 'the one who started all of this in the first place—'

'It was Jacob,' Holly admitted, knowing it was too late now to continue the cover-up. 'Just back from New Orleans.'

'Tall, dimpled, nice smell?' Beth shook her head. 'I should have known. See, I told you that first day it was kismet, and you didn't believe me.'

'I do now.'

'You do?' Beth laid a slight hand on Holly's arm. 'You love him, don't you?'

'I do, Beth. Stupid me, I really do.' Holly leant into her friend's warm embrace finally feeling lost, but with that came enormous relief as now she could hopefully begin to find a way out. Now she had said it aloud she wouldn't have to shoulder the load on her own.

'You're not stupid. It's natural.'

'But he doesn't love me,' Holly said between gulping breaths as she swallowed back the tears that threatened to spill.

'I wouldn't know about that. I know for a fact he has spent the whole evening watching you and Derek with a great scowl on his face.'

'I was mean to him.'

Beth laughed. 'He's a big boy. He can handle mean.'

'Then he feels sorry for me.'

'Well, maybe he does. And maybe he just cares.'

'That's the very worst part. I don't think he does. I think he has spent a lifetime cultivating the ability not to care. And, like everything he puts his mind to, he is very good at it.'

'So do all these latest philosophies complement your

grand theory about men and marriage or are we putting
that behind us now?'

'Way, way behind us. The whole thing showed cracks
from day one. Yet I kept insisting Ben take me on the hunt
as I tweaked and fine-tuned along the way to suit my own
capricious wishes. Oh, Beth. I am so sorry. I feel like the
last three weeks have slipped through my fingertips. It's
all been a total waste.'

Beth pulled Holly back up straight and wiped two soft
fingers under her welling eyes.

'It hasn't all been a waste. You put on a great party. So,
enjoy that success. We can sort the rest of your life out
tomorrow.'

Holly nodded, and Beth gave her a kiss on the cheek
before leaving her to tidy up.

The party was still in full swing. No matter what, the
evening had been a marvellous success. The plates had
been licked clean. Not a soul had yet left. And the dance
floor was packed. But as Holly moved towards the solitude
of the balcony, no matter how hard she rationalised that
this was all she should have hoped for, her heart wished
for a great deal more.

Once outside, she had barely had time to take a deep
breath of the crisp evening air when she heard the glass
door slide open and close behind her. It was Derek.

'Go back inside, Derek. I won't be long.'

Without saying a word, he came up behind her and
wrapped his arms around her waist.

'Derek, please! What are you doing?' she yelled as she
struggled to free herself from his grasp.

He spun her around roughly. There was hidden strength
in his thin arms. 'We're grown-ups, Holly. Don't pretend
you don't know what I am doing. Why else would you

ask me out after all this time?' His hands gripped her under her arms, his bony fingers digging into her flesh.

'No, Derek! I just thought you might like a night out with people you knew.'

'And you thought I might make Mr Lincoln jealous.'

Holly stopped struggling and looked up into Derek's leering eyes, stunned at his perception.

'I'm no fool, Holly. I saw the way he looked at you with unsatisfied desire. I know that feeling well enough to recognise it in a fellow man. And I figure the way to do my good deed, to make him properly jealous, is to do to you what he obviously has not yet managed.'

Derek pushed Holly back against the hard metal railing, bruising her spine, pinning her so close she could not reach her hands in between them to push him away. She beat furiously at his hunched back as he ravaged her neck with rough, biting kisses.

'No! Derek, stop. Please!'

Before Holly needed to say another word Derek was wrenched away from her. Through her tousled hair she watched Derek cower with his hands over his face. A fist swung from Derek's left and landed on his jaw with crunching impact. He spun around and crumpled to the ground landing spread-eagled, almost on top of her feet.

Holly gasped and sprang back. Her eyes swung up to meet Derek's aggressor.

Jacob stood, feet shoulder-width apart, his head held high, rubbing his right fist with his left palm. His eyes were bright and his nostrils flared with each ragged breath.

Holly herself was slack-jawed, panting, and dry-mouthed and she could not draw her eyes away from the potent sight before her.

Jacob took one step forward to make sure she was okay. Holly flinched only slightly at his sudden movement but it was enough to stop him dead in his tracks. His eyes softened and his throat worked with several uneasy swallows.

'Jacob. I...thank you. I mean, he was...' She desperately fought back the tears that were threatening to spill now that her adrenalin rush was dissipating. 'He was determined. If you hadn't have come out when you did—'

'I know. You don't have to say it,' Jacob whispered, the confusion and worry etched on his beautiful face.

'I'm...I'm fine,' Holly insisted, her tears now flowing freely.

'Holly.' The word wrenched from Jacob's straining vocal cords. 'Please let me come to you. I need to know you are not hurt.'

She held up a hand so that he would keep his distance; she was shaking enough without having to deal with him standing so close, looking at her like that. Then she looked down at Derek's prone figure. And she stood outside her own raw emotions for a moment and realised he hadn't moved a muscle since he'd dropped.

'Jacob, you knocked him out cold. With one punch.'

'I know.'

'You're a trained fighter. He could sue you for assault and he would probably win.'

'Do you think he *should* win such a case?'

'I think you have had so much practice and experience and you have such innate passion, Jacob, and I'm not sure that you can control it.'

'Hell, Holly, do you have any idea what I could have done to Derek if I had the inclination to punish him and not just to get him away from you? But more importantly do you have any real idea of where my passion is directed? Where it has been directed for the last weeks? Where I wish more than anything else in the world it was directed right now?'

She had stopped breathing, suddenly acutely aware of the fresh evening breeze caressing every single hair on her bare arms. A sprinkling of sensitive goose-bumps sprang up and a sensuous shiver quaked through her from top to toe.

As though instinctively sensing her surrender, Jacob stepped over the prostrate payroll clerk in one swift move and gathered her, pliant and ready, into his arms. She melted against him instantaneously, all of her anxiety and fear dissolving in his protective embrace. Their lips met in a crushing and desperate kiss as though they were unlucky lovers who had been waiting a lifetime to consummate their obsession.

Her arms wrapped around his neck relishing the sensation his soft, springy hair created over her sensitised fingertips. His arms wrapped tight around her back, brushing over the spot where the railing had only moments before bruised her. But his strong hands felt like a balm, a warm, sure comfort against all her hurts. Holly stood on tiptoe and Jacob curved against her so that they could be as close as could be whilst still standing up.

The kiss found its own fervent rhythm as tongues and lips melded in one great fierce, hot union that both bruised and mollified the pair. They squeezed together tighter, needing and gaining from each other a sense of unity and belonging and devotion.

'Holly?' a voice queried from the doorway.

Holly and Jacob leapt apart as thought hit by a bolt of electricity. Holly instinctively tried to pull away and straighten herself out but Jacob looked down upon her kindly before planting one last kiss on the tip of her nose.

Lydia and Ana stood in the doorway, looking from them

to the unconscious Derek, their mouths hanging open in matching 'O's.

'Lydia,' Jacob said calmly, 'could you please bring Dr Thomas out to check on Derek here? He is unconscious, but with some smelling salts he should be fine. Unfortunately there will be no lasting damage bar a rather nasty headache.'

'Ah, I would get Dr Thomas but he is otherwise engaged with Beth,' Lydia explained, her eyes wide and glued to the man on the ground.

'Beth?' Holly stepped forward and grabbed Lydia by the arms. 'What's wrong with Beth, Lydia?'

'Nothing's wrong,' Lydia promised. 'She's just having her baby. That's all.'

JACOB ran down the hospital hallway alone, and rounded the corner to find Ben and Holly clinging to one another in a tight embrace. He stopped his run so abruptly his shoes screeched loudly on the linoleum floor. But neither of them even noticed.

'I'm petrified, Holly.' Jacob could hear Ben's strained voice.

He watched as they pulled apart and winced as he saw that Holly kept hold of Ben's hands. 'Don't be. She's stronger than the two of us put together.'

'Should I go in yet?' Ben asked. 'Do you think they are waiting for me?'

Jacob waited for Holly's endearment, for a profession of her feelings. Knowing it could not possibly be true, but petrified into inaction just the same. But then she let go of Ben and ran two rough hands over his hair, messing it up so badly the worry left his face and he relaxed with laughter.

'Ben,' Holly said, 'I'm sure this baby is not waiting for even you. Go get 'em, tiger.'

A nurse came through the swinging doors and took Ben through to the maternity rooms.

And Jacob realized that what Holly had said was true. There was nothing more between her and Ben than affection. He felt a great weight lift off his shoulders. When he had accused Holly of secretly loving Ben, he had been searching for a fault, for a reason not to feel the intense affection for her that had grown so rapidly since he had first spotted her.

But just now, watching her play down her own worries for Beth to give all of her consideration to a friend in need, he knew there was no reason to be worrying.

He swallowed down the tender lump that had formed in his throat. He so wanted to reach out and take her in his own arms and make sure that *she* was the one feeling fine.

As though finally sensing Jacob was there, Holly drifted over towards him like metal to a magnet. He held out an arm, she came to him, and he gathered her close to his chest. And it felt so right. Never before had he felt safe and protective all at once. And rather than sending him running to the far reaches of the earth, there was nowhere else he wanted to be.

But his pleasure was short-lived as Ana, Michael and Lydia arrived. Jacob watched helpless as Lydia wrenched Holly from his arms and hung onto her like a baby limpet. And even with Ana and Michael tugging on his arm and barraging him with questions and attention, he felt alone. And he knew just what he needed to make that feeling go away.

A couple of hours later, Ana, Michael and Lydia had fallen asleep. Lydia had curled up in a big armchair, her feet tucked beneath her. Ana's head rested in Michael's lap and his hand lay protectively in her hair where he had been stroking her until he too had nodded off.

Holly glanced at Jacob to find him watching her. His hair was dishevelled, his face tired, he looked so much as he had that first morning not so long ago. No wonder she had been instantly smitten. He was so artlessly captivating, especially in those rare moments when his guard was down. She licked her dry lips and ran a hand over her hair, suddenly wishing she had a comb and a compact and a tub of lip-gloss at hand.

'Come with me to grab a coffee,' Jacob whispered, his low, smooth voice echoing faintly across the spacious room. 'I want to talk to you about something.'

'Shouldn't we stay? I want to be here in case something happens.'

'It will only take a few minutes. We can bring some coffee back for these guys who will soon need something and I can't carry them all on my own.'

Holly nodded. She peeled herself from her chair, making sure not to disturb the others.

In silence she followed him into the lift. What was so important Jacob wanted to talk to her about it, now of all times? It couldn't be about the job offer. That would be so inappropriate. Maybe he was going to tell her he was leaving again. She shuddered at the thought, and obviously mistaking her action Jacob shrugged off his suit jacket and lay it softly around her bare shoulders.

She smiled her thanks, careful to contain the absolute love she felt for him at such a kind gesture.

They exited the lift and she followed him into the all-night cafeteria. They ordered a couple of take-away coffees and found a table in a quiet corner by the window.

Holly sipped on her coffee and waited for Jacob to talk, more nervous than she had ever been in her whole life.

'I wanted to apologise.'

'What for this time?' She tried to keep her voice light.

'For the suggestions I made about you and Ben.'

'Oh.' Wow. That wasn't what she had expected at all. 'Well, thank you.'

'I know now why you chose Ben. You were looking for a type that he represented, someone dependable. I understand that.'

Jacob was looking down at his hands. They were wringing the life out of the edge of the tablecloth.

'I didn't see all that before, because, you see, I...I was jealous.'

Her heart sang. *Jealous?*

'I didn't want you turning to him for answers when I felt like you should have been turning to me.'

Her heart sank. 'To find me dates?'

'Hell no!' He raked a forceful hand through his sexily unkempt hair. 'That was the last thing I wanted you to be doing. Running about with every Tom, Derek and Matt.'

'The last thing you *wanted*?' *Please, Jacob, please tell me what I want to hear.*

He locked gazes with her, his expression pained, as if he had gone through the wringer. It mirrored Holly's own feelings exactly. Holly did not look away. Could not.

'It's the last thing I *want*.'

Was he really saying what she hoped so desperately he was saying? This was the moment she had to make sure. One way or the other.

'Then what do you want?' Her voice sounded as though it were coming from a great distance away.

He looked deep into her eyes, so intensely her knees threatened to melt under the heat.

'You.'

He wanted her! He really wanted her. But was that enough? She loved him. And if he did not love her back with the same force and hopefulness, it would never be enough. Unable to voice a single sensible thought, she kept quiet and let him speak.

'The minute Ben told me that you were on a husband hunt,' Jacob continued, 'I pictured myself in the role. Whereas the thought had always brought me out in a nasty rash before, I felt this sense of ease wash over me, like I had been waiting to picture myself in that role all my life. Well, it has driven me around the bend. I can't sleep, I'm barely eating and no matter how hard I try I cannot keep my thoughts or my hands off you. What do you think we should do about it?'

You tell me, she thought, but her throat was too tight with emotion to say the words.

'Well, I've had plenty of sleepless nights to think about it and I have come up with a solution.'

He paused, only long enough to unwrap his hands from the tablecloth and smooth them on top of hers. He enclosed his warm palms around hers, the sensation creating waves of heavenly heat along her arms.

'Marry me.'

'What?' Holly squeaked, loud enough to turn a few nurses' heads.

'Marry me, Holly.'

'But…why?'

He rolled his eyes comically. 'Why not? Why shouldn't a man madly and hopelessly in love propose marriage?'

'Madly? And hopelessly…?'

'In love. Because that's what I am, Holly. You hardly gave me much choice, turning up everywhere I went, never letting me forget for a second what a talent and a whirlwind and a knockout you truly are.'

'You turned up everywhere I went—'

'Either way, every time I thought I had managed to rationalise my growing feelings away, there you were, so beautiful and charming and absolutely lovable. I had no chance.' He smiled at her, his dimples growing deeper as his eyes softened. 'Then at last I realised I did not want the chance not to love you. I wanted the chance to love you more than anything else in the world.'

'Oh, Jacob. I had no idea.'

'I realised as much. So all it took was a horrifically expensive party to prove it to you. Then I found this great last-minute ski holiday deal and encouraged Ana and Michael to go.'

It slowly dawned on her what he meant.

'You sent Ana away?'

'Well, they were planning on going away anyway—they just weren't planning on going quite so soon.'

'So I would have to organise the party with you?'

'Uh-huh. I told you I buy my way into the women in my life's affections. But then you had to go and spoil it all by not coming to the party with me. That was not part of the grand plan.'

She blushed for the first time, though her confidence was soaring sky-high. 'My turn to apologise?'

'I should think so. You could have at least picked someone like Matt Riley to flaunt in front of me. Feeling envious of a man like Derek Gordon does not do much for a man's ego.'

Holly buried her face in her palms. 'Please don't remind me. That was not one of my more sensible plans.'

'As opposed to husband-hunting all because some oaf in the street gave you a bit of lip?'

Holly dropped her hands to the table.

'How did you know? Ben! Did Ben tell you? Or was it Beth? I knew she would not keep out of it. Lydia? It was Lydia wasn't it? That girl cannot keep her mouth shut—'

'What does it matter now?' he asked. 'I have been smitten with you since before I knew that juicy bit of info, though how could it not help?'

He grinned and Holly slapped him on the arm. He caught her hand and brought it to his mouth for a soft, tender kiss.

'The truth is, ever since I spotted those ridiculous yellow

galoshes covering up your breathtaking legs I have been yours for the taking, Ms Holly Denison.'

'At the greyhound race?' she asked, her eyes riveted on her hand where he continued to rain short, sweet kisses.

'Mmm hmm. To see a woman like you, a woman with such finesse and such class, happily slap on a pair of rubber boots to help an old man out of a fix, in that moment, I was gone.'

He had loved her for so long. Since before she had told him about her pitiable childhood. All that time he had been protective and supportive because he loved her, not because he felt badly for her. It was too wonderful.

That was more than she needed to hear to dump her cup and leap from her chair onto his lap. She buried her face in his neck, running a spray of kisses across his chin and face and then onto his heavenly waiting mouth. All too soon he pulled away, though she clung, determined never to let him go again.

'What do you have to say for yourself, Ms Denison?'

Finally unwilling and unable to hide her intense feelings, she let the love shine through her eyes. 'I love you with all my heart and soul, Jacob Lincoln.'

He rolled his eyes to the heavens. 'Well, that much I knew already.'

She stared in shock.

'Haven't you been told you have the most useless poker-face?'

Holly could do nothing but continue to gape.

'I mean, Ms Denison. You haven't answered my pressing question.'

She couldn't answer him yet, though her heart screamed the answer out so loud she could hardly think straight.

'Jacob, I adore you to the bottom of my heart. But I could not live with myself if because of me you felt

trapped. You once told me you refuse to get bogged down
in just one project—'

'You are not a project, Holly. You are the woman I love.
It's true that I spent my adult life convincing myself I
wanted to be free, but it was a false freedom because I
carried my own wall with me everywhere I went. Then
you came along equipped with just the steps I needed to
get over that wall.'

His voice was low, lilting, and indulgent and made her
light-headed as well as light-hearted.

'It took you three weeks to climb a bunch of steps?'

'It was a tall wall.' He punctuated his words with a trail
of soft, warm kisses across her shoulder and she had to
force herself to stay on track.

'But my hunt for a husband, that must have planted the
idea in your head from the outset—'

'Holly, will you just shut up? This is my final offer.
Take it or leave it.'

She shut up.

'Work with me at Lincoln Holdings. Live with me at
your place or mine, I don't care which. If I decide to go
away, it will only be with you at my side. But above all
things, marry me. That I'm afraid is the clincher in this
deal.'

'But, I thought you would only hire me if I wasn't married.'

He stared at her in bewilderment. 'Now how on earth
did that silly idea get stuck in that beautiful head of yours?'

'At Lunar, when you were hounding me about playing
my cards right, I thought you were intimating you would
not be keen on hiring someone with plans to become pregnant.'

Jacob reached up and ran his agile fingers through a
loose tendril of Holly's hair. 'So you have plans to become

pregnant, do you? Well, if you have *plans*, then who am I to argue? I'm convinced! I think we should put aside several days, maybe even weeks to focus on nothing but this plan of yours.'

Holly all but swooned. It took all of her remaining wits to gather her strength for one last important question. 'And, by the way, what are you going to do to Lunar?'

'Marry me and you can have the damn place as a wedding present.' He grabbed her around the waist and leaned in so she could taste his warm breath on her lips. 'You talk too much, woman. Yet I have still not heard the one word I am looking for.'

But before she could put him out of his misery he proceeded to stop her talking in the tenderest manner possible.

'Mr Lincoln? Ms Denison?' a nurse called out from the far end of the room.

They both turned, though this time Holly kept a tight hold of her man.

'Mr Jeffries is looking for you.'

'Is everything all right?' Holly asked.

The nurse smiled. 'Everything's fine. They would love you to come and meet their new baby daughter.'

Holly looked to Jacob and saw his eyes were glistening with emotion.

'A daughter,' he whispered. 'A daughter who will be loved and cared for by two wonderful parents.'

'And two thoroughly devoted godparents.'

Holly leaned in and lightly kissed away his beautiful tears.

Holly leant over her friend, who woke up from a quick nap.

'Holly, you're here.'

'Of course I'm here, you numbskull.'

'And Jacob?'

'He's here too.'

Jacob moved away from his position at the doorway and joined Holly, laying a hand on her shoulder.

'We saw her,' he said, his voice thick with emotion, 'and she's beautiful.'

'But she looks nothing like Ben,' Holly joked.

'I thought the same thing,' Beth said with a weak smile. 'But don't tell him that; he thinks she's his spitting image. What he doesn't guess won't hurt him.'

Holly nodded and Jacob winked conspiratorially. Beth's heavy eyes glanced from Holly, who was still wearing Jacob's suit jacket, to Jacob, whose hand was now lightly playing with Holly's hair, and her smile turned to a grin.

'You two look like the cats who got the cream.'

'You're not the only one with good news tonight,' Holly said.

'Really? What's the news? Who has news?'

'We do.'

'Well, come on, don't leave an exhausted woman on tenterhooks, I'll as likely fall asleep before you tell me as not.'

Holly looked to Jacob and felt herself glowing under his adoring gaze. He nodded at her, a loving smile radiating down upon her as he gave her shoulder a supportive squeeze. Holly dragged her eyes from the man she loved to face her beloved friend, and said:

'I'm getting married.'

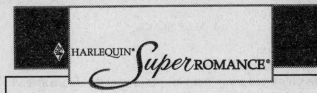

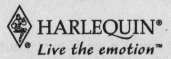

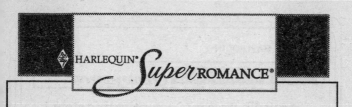

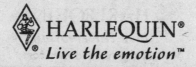

HARLEQUIN®

AMERICAN *Romance®*

proudly presents a captivating new miniseries by bestselling author

Cathy Gillen Thacker

THE BRIDES OF HOLLY SPRINGS

Weddings are serious business in the picturesque town of Holly Springs! The sumptuous Wedding Inn—the only place to go for the splashiest nuptials in this neck of the woods—is owned and operated by matriarch Helen Hart. This no-nonsense Steel Magnolia has also single-handedly raised five studly sons and one feisty daughter, so now all that's left is whipping up weddings for her beloved offspring....

Don't miss the first four installments:

THE VIRGIN'S SECRET MARRIAGE
December 2003

THE SECRET WEDDING WISH
April 2004

THE SECRET SEDUCTION
June 2004

PLAIN JANE'S SECRET LIFE
August 2004

Available at your favorite retail outlet.

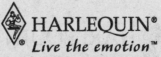

HARLEQUIN®

Live the emotion™

Visit us at www.eHarlequin.com

HARHS

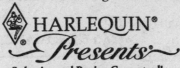

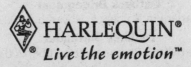